SHERLOCK HOLMES

AND

A HOLE IN THE DEVIL'S TAIL

(A Narrative of Dr. John Watson)

By Viktor Messick

Paperback ISBN 978-1-78705-018-1
ePub ISBN 978-1-78705-019-8
PDF ISBN 978-1-78705-020-4

Published in the UK by MX Publishing
335 Princess Park Manor, Royal Drive, London, N11 3GX
www.mxpublishing.co.uk

Cover design by Brian Belanger.

Dedicated to my inner circle: Annie, Nala, Henry and Cecil.

Chapter 1

The Gantlet is Thrown Down

Early evening tea is always an agreeable occasion, but especially pleasant on a Sunday. This is due to the fact that the holiest day of the week, by way of inviolable law (enacted with the best of intentions, I am certain) passes the slowest and consequently in the least stimulating fashion. Such was the case on a particular Sabbath day in March of 189-, corresponding with the outbreak of the horrific London Tarot Murders, an episode occupying a lofty place in the annals of all black deeds ever committed in the long memory of the ancient, regal city, higher even than the infamous affair with the Ripper. I recall the day being a principally uneventful, melancholy sort, gray and windless. I loafed about my apartment all morning and visited a recuperating friend in the afternoon, returning home at the onset of dreary twilight, bearing the angst of a man who has exhausted all serious business far before the day is spent. Upon my return, I recall perusing, for the third or fourth time that day, a thumbed copy of that morning's edition, then, for the second or third time, reading a mildly interesting letter from a friend of mine who ran a missionary school near the banks of the Krishna in Kamataka. Try as I might to keep my mind occupied, however, the boredom became unbearable, and my humor suffered.

My mood, I should note, did steadily improve as the small hand of the clock dial approached its middle station, an occurrence which invariably coincided with

Mrs. Hudson, my gracious landlady, appearing through the door bearing a silver tray with steaming teapot along with warm scones, as well as fresh copies of the evening Times, all for the pleasure and amusement of myself and my esteemed companion and fellow lodger, Mr. Sherlock Holmes.

As the hues of night gathered, the kind lady made her timely entrance with her faithful tray. A lamp was lighted at our backs, and with its steady brilliance behind us and the glow of the fire in the grate before us, we were afforded ample light for our long evening of digesting all the printed news at our disposal. I reached first for the edible contents, my friend for the inedible, namely a white envelope which sat atop one of the copies of the paper, an act quite justifiable as it bore his name upon it in letters black and bold. As I watched, he silently read its contents, then, after indulging in a small, private laugh, he turned his attention to the paper.

"Two more tarot murders, Watson," said my friend a few moments later. "These done in by clubbing. Nasty business."

"Holmes, please," I protested, not yet half way through my buttery pastry. The previous day's paper had been sufficiently graphic as to leave me unnerved. It recounted the mutilated condition in which the first two tarot murder victims were found. There was reported in the same edition a second grisly crime, an equally appalling narrative involving the demise of one Mr. Richard Corkright, a lawyer found strangled in his

Merton office with a bloated white face and deep red welts around his neck. Such accounts of man's inhumanity to man are sufficient to compel even the most hardened heart to wonder at the state of the world.

My friend went on, paying my plea not the slightest heed."The three and four of rods were found on them, apparently from the same Italian deck previously used. You recall, Watson? The brothers Newquist found yesterday, mercilessly stabbed and left with Il Uni di Spades and Il Due di Spades pinned to their faces. Strangely (or perhaps appropriately) the two latest victims were also brothers, Larry and Robert Dornbeck the unfortunates' names."

Annoyed at Holmes' insensitivity, I patiently finished my confectionary treat before responding.

"I'm afraid such events are more unnerving than amusing to us regular citizens. You, I'm sure, are fascinated with the particulars."

"Quite so, Watson. Quite so," said Holmes from behind his paper.

"It does, however, present you with a sore dilemma."

"A dilemma, you said, Watson?" quoth my friend innocently.

"Yes, Holmes," I answered. "Lacking time to pursue two investigations, you are forced to choose between the Corkright case and that of the Tarot murders."

The paper came down in a flash and I beheld my friend's smiling countenance. "Ah, there you err, my dear Watson, for my time is plenteous, with very little occupying it. No inviting prospects in the concert halls nor in the small theatres which I frequent. My assistance has already been officially requested by Inspector McVay concerning the Merton murder. And, with regard to the so-called tarot murders, well, the gauntlet has been thrown down!"

He tossed me a folded piece of paper, which I knew to be the very note contained in the alabaster envelope found atop Mrs. Hudson's tray. The contents were in beautiful old-English calligraphy.

Dearest Sir! [ran the note]

This correspondence is written by the hand of one more versed in your unrefined Germanic oriented language, but be assured that the sentiments are mine. I know you are a man not easily intimidated. I respect this. Nay, my good Sir, I admire it to the highest degree. As a gentleman I must inform you, however, that if you decide to meddle in MY affairs, as I fear the magnificent Sherlock Holmes might feel compelled to do, I give my solemn vow to inflict a vengeance horrible and unholy, not upon your distinguished person, but rather upon the lives of those you most cherish. I go about the Earth doing the work of a Higher Authority, handing out judgments reached in celestial courts far above the mortal world. My work is sacred - divine in its own right - and I will suffer no interference. As this evening's paper will attest, I am a man dedicated to a solemn and severe calling. As this missive is penned, a third and fourth tarot card have just been assigned, and more cards remain at my disposal! The King of Terrors shall receive those against whom I set my will. He Who Shall Not Be Cheated! You have been warned!"

Most Sincerely,

The Tarot Master

"So, you see, Watson," rejoined my friend, "Professional obligation necessitates the one investigation, personal honor the other. I thus have little choice but to divide my attention between the two cases."

I frowned, the words of the note lingering in my mind like the musk of an unpleasant odor

"This note is the product of a deranged mind! Aren't you the least bit concerned?"

"It is not my safety that has been threatened, Watson, but that of my only close relation, my brother Mycroft, and my only true friend, you. Men of my trade pursue their treasure well aware of the perils by which it must be won and think little of their own security. I will, however, suffer no harm to come to those I hold dear. Thus the villain wisely threatens their lives and not mine."

I complacently leaned back in my chair. "Well, I refuse to be intimidated."

My companion clapped his hands. "Exactly what I would expect John Watson to say! And I have no doubt that Mycroft Holmes would echo it. Therefore, I am inclined to proceed."

"You have some competition this time," I noted, having picked up my copy of the paper and perused it. "Says here that the 'Friends of Richard Corkright' are putting together a fund. A cash payment is to be paid for information leading to the capture of his murderer and the return of all stolen items."

At this, the great detective became somewhat agitated. "Oh, Watson, do you really suppose me to be intimidated by amateurish crime solving methods involving talentless competitors? No, no. I shall enjoy a good sleep tonight and venture out to Merton tomorrow, bright and early. I would enjoy your company, if you are available."

Fortunately, I was. The mixed feelings which these cases of Holmes inspire me, however, served to somewhat diminish the gaiety I felt upon noticing my companion, lost in the articles of the Daily, had left his pastry unclaimed. I helped myself, but before I had quite devoured it, my friend resumed our conversation.

"And how is that poem you're working on coming along?"

The astonishment manifested on my face was reflected in the sly smile of my friend.

"I began it last night in my room. I am sure that the door was closed. How could you possibly know of it!"

Holmes Shrugged. "You told me, albeit not in words. I have noted the past two days that you have neglected to take any milk at breakfast, in violation of your usual practice. Such deviations, I have come to note, coincide with occasions on which you have indulged (a less diplomatic person might say overindulged) in cheese. I know for a fact that your favorite cheese is Danish, which you almost always purchase from Vitskol's over on Zealand Street, which is near Isidore's Bookshop, which you invariably visit after purchasing your cheese. Your favorite activity at Isidore's is to examine the collections of poetry, and, more often than not, when John Watson reads poetry he is inspired to make an attempt at emulating it. Now, come, my friend, and do share your masterpiece with me."

"I would rather show you the complete work," I balked.

"You disappoint me, Watson," returned my friend good-naturedly. "But, as you like."

And thus we both of us quietly turned our undivided attention to the paper.

Chapter 2

A Visit to the Murder Room

Early the next day we made our way to Merton. The path to the office of the late Richard Corkright was a relatively strait one and none too far, but Fate conspired to delay us. Just as we entered that parish, traffic came to standstill. Both Holmes and myself left our cab to investigate the cause of the obstruction. We found that a dairy wagon had somehow overturned at a nearby intersection. Too impatient to wait for the situation to be rectified, we decided to pursue our destination on foot. The sky above us was a foreboding shade, one that threatened rain. With an according inclination toward speed, we set down the sidewalk.

Not two blocks had we gained when another obstacle presented itself, this in the form of a shabby man, surely between fifty-five and sixty, popping up in front of us. He tipped his hat, but Holmes and I paid him no heed, for we were too preoccupied in achieving our destination. I went to his left, Holmes to his right. Not to be easily deterred, however, the man began walking along side us, straining to keep up. With effort, he spoke to us.

"Excuse the liberty, gentlemen, but might I trouble you a bit."

"If you're about begging, you might not," I answered him bluntly. "We're on important business."

He continued to follow us.

"So I sees, sir. So I sees," he answered me. "I was hoping there might be some small service I might render you nice Christian gentlemen in exchange for the price of a loaf of bread."

"Ha! In exchange for a bit to spend at the tavern I'd wager."

The man laughed kindly at my remark. "I'm sorry to say you'd lose that wager, sir! Aye, I used to bend the elbow as much as any bloke – maybe more so - but now I'm a family man again. I gave up the devil brew when my daughter and her little child came to live with me in my humble place down toward the River Wandle just last month. All I gets goes toward their keep."

"Really, Watson, the fastest way to expedite these situations is the sacrifice of a shilling." Holmes tossed the man a coin. He stopped to catch it. We continued.

Then, to my great surprise (and I suspect to Holmes as well), the man again dogged us.

"Thank you kindly, sir," he addressed Holmes, "But I meant what I said and I'd much prefer to earn my bob. Perhaps I can guide you to where you need to go? I know these parts rather well I do."

To my amazement, Holmes stopped and turned to face the man. He stated the street name and asked if the man could guide us there. The man's face brightened.

"Get you to McGeady Street, sir! I can get you there in less than half of an hour! I swear on that there holy book."

He indicated the tome in Holmes' hand, an Italian dictionary Holmes had brought with him to read during the trip.

"You think that a Bible do you?" I asked.

"Never mind that, Watson. Look here, Mr...."

"Broadnax they call me, sir."

"Mr. Broadnax, we would be most grateful if you would take us to our destination with dispatch."

The old fellow picked up at this command. "Yes, sir! Right away, sir! Off to High street we go.

He set off, now Holmes and I seeking to keep up with him.

I tapped the man on his shoulder. "High Street? The address we seek in 14 McGeady?" The man half-bowed in apology.

"Pardon me, sir, around these parts we seldom call it by its proper name but instead call it The High Street as it runs over us and is inhabited by men of a, shall we say, a higher station than ourselves. You gentlemen will no doubt notice the road dipping down. High Street will come into our view shortly. Up there. It's called by many other names, which I won't repeat before gentlemen such as yourselves."

"Have you so much time to think of mocking names for that place of honest commerce?" I found this intelligence vexing.

"It's hard not to think of that there place, looking down on us, as it were. The shadows of its taller buildings circling around our feet all the day long. Might I ask what business you gentlemen have there?"

It was my friend who answered.

"We're to visit a friend. Richard Cockright."

Our guide stopped.

"Blimey but ain't you heard, sir! I'm sorry to have to tell you that gentleman's dead. Killed last Friday in his office. Great mystery how the killer got in and out. Some of the blokes thought it was funny when the news went around about the chuffed red haired lawyer being knocked in his own place. I didn't find no humor in it."

"Nor should you have," I chimed in.

Holmes took the man by the elbow, set him walking again.

"We are perfectly aware of what happened. What can you tell us of the deceased gentleman?"

"Me, sir? Not much. Just what's in the paper that my daughter reads to me, or what I hears others talk about. I can tell you this much, sir: there's whispering going 'round about that murder."

"Whispering, Mr. Broadnax?"

"Well, sir, - we can take this here way, gentleman, that's it - well, sir, as I was about to say, some believe that it was them Shrike brothers that is responsible for the black deed."

I asked him to whom he was referring, but it was Holmes who answered me.

"The Shrike brothers, Watson. A criminal gang ran by four brothers that used to operate in these parts, specifically in the vicinity of Avebury. They were taken down by the police months ago. Tried and hung."

Our guide was becoming a bit winded, but devoutly led us on. There were short spaces between each of his sentences.

"Aye, sir, you recall correctly. And it wasn't really the police as caught 'em, sir, begging your pardon. The police weren't quite up to the task, (them Shrikes were the clever type!) and so a bounty was put together by some of the merchants up on High street and some young fellows rounded 'em up and handed 'em over to the constabulary, who were mighty glad to get their hands on 'em. The brothers went to the scaffolding and most of their boys to cells."

"But if the brothers are dead and the gang disbanded, who is suspected of enacting the revenge?" I asked.

"There were others who sympathized with 'em. Some of them young blockheads who listened to the lectures the brothers' gave in the south-side taverns some nights."

"Lectures? Does this make any sense to you, Holmes?"

"Perfect sense, Watson. You see, the Shrike brothers were not run of the mill criminals, but what you might call provocateurs, spouting the doctrines of Mills and Marx and the like."

"Mischievous rebel rousers!" I commented.

"As you say, sir," said our guide, I think to get our attention, for our path was just then to change. "Hope you gentlemen don't mind winding down this here alley. Or perhaps I should say winding up this here alley."

The way indicated soon became quite steep and rather untidy (as alleys are want to be). I hesitated.

"Surely there is a way more...negotiable."

Our guide laughed politely.

"There might be, sir. But I understood you gentlemen to be somewhat of a hurry."

"If it's the quickest, then this is fine, my good fellow," said Holmes.

"Oh, it is, sir. Ain't no quicker way than the Devil's Tail."

"The Devil's Tail?" I queried.

"So they calls it, sir. Since before my time."

"Seems to be getting narrower by the step," I noted.

"Aye, it does, sir. Mind your step, gentlemen. Yes, these rows of buildings on both side 'ave been built and rebuilt many a time over the years and each time they seems to expand out into the alley space, so that over time the alley has been somewhat narrowed and curvy shaped."

The space between the borders gradually dwindled to the point where we practically brushed our shoulders against the alley wall. Not easily deterred, we nevertheless pressed on. Our guide struggled to keep his old, pinched form in front of us, managing to just do so.

Forfeiting only a small degree of what is our usual speed, Holmes and I successfully negotiated the length of the slim, sinuous alley with minimal delay, and, reaching its termination, ventured around a tight corner to find ourselves on a posh London street. With a bit of ceremony, our faithful guide announced the conclusion of his commission.

"Here we are, gentlemen. quick as 'ole Broadnax could get you here! He knows his onions, by gar! Ain't as fast as I once was, nor as slow as many men over half a century in age."

Somewhere toward the end of these rambling declarations, (and perhaps with the objective of hastening them to some sort of conclusion) my companion extended his hand toward our guide. The old man took it with honor, and, retracting it, found himself in possession of another shilling. He stared at it with half-suppressed joy.

"Oh, but, sir, don't you recall that you already paid me?"

"A bonus for speedy service," responded Holmes succinctly.

The man bowed. "Yes, sir. Thank you, sir! Lord bless your kindness, sir!" He tipped his hat at us, continuing to express his gratitude to us even after we turned our backs upon him and gave him no more attention.

The neighborhood before us was of a refined commercial nature, though presently remarkably vacant - possessing, in fact, an almost imposing emptiness. It lay at the end of a street which curved rather sharply in its termination, affording its residents a high degree of solitude for a public road. It seemed a neighborhood in mourning.

A steady rain began falling down upon us and we promptly found the office once inhabited by the deceased solicitor. It turned out to be situated between the office of a funeral parlor and a South American importing company. Our beacon was the presence of a uniformed police officer keeping vigil at its threshold. My companioned hailed the man as we approached.

"Good morning, officer. I am Sherlock Holmes. This is my companion Dr. Watson."

The young man seemed a statue. He barely acknowledged us.

"I believe instructions were left for you regarding us."

"No instructions, sir," said the flippant fellow. "My orders is to keep out everybody ain't a policeman."

I became angry at this effrontery. "Come, my good man," I protested. "Did you not hear this gentleman's name? Do you not know of the esteem with which your superiors hold him? Is it possible you've not heard of all the assistance he's rendered in the past?"

My friend held up his hand.

"Enough, Watson," he said. "The lad but does his duty. There's been a mistake. Let us pay a visit to police headquarters and clear matters up."

Such a trip, however, proved to be unnecessary, for at that moment footsteps could be heard from the street before us. We turned to behold, through the large drops of rain running off the slanted roof above us, two hunched over figures approaching. One man, barely middle aged I'd say, was a constable, while the other gentleman, more advanced in years, sported a dark grey overcoat over a sharp brown tweed suit. Both were strangers to me.

"Haybert, you imbecile," cried the policeman to his colleague. "Are you keeping these here gentlemen waiting? Move aside, lunkhead!"

The young man before us became immediately flustered, his face taking on some umber. "Begging your pardon, sir, I was told to admit no one."

"Well, I've just come from the office of Inspector McVay and he says to let these men in, as their helping with his investigation. You stand down or answer to him!" He returned to a civil tone before addressing us. "Begging your pardon, gentlemen. Inspector McVay sends his regards. This here is Mr. Peter De Greek, secretary to the late Mr. Corkright, who was kind enough to come. He can show you around the premises and answer any questions you may have. Mr. De Greek, sir, this is Mr. Holmes and Dr. Watson."

With a quick salute, the constable was off. The reproached guardian moved aside, and we followed Mr. De Greek as he, with his stately tread, lead us past the door and into the darkened office of his late employer.

"May I inquire as to how long you served Mr. Corkright?" asked Holmes.

"I am proud to have served Mr. Corkright for the better half of two decades, sir."

"Quite a record of service."

He dismissed the commendation with a wave of his hand.

"None to speak of. My master took me in when no other employer would have spared a second glance. Later, when my reputation spread, other offers were placed before me. But here I stayed, at my post, and have never wasted one regretful thought. A man should stay where he is happy, Mr. Holmes. This here, gentlemen, is, the lobby, of course. Here is my desk. And here is my late benefactor." The last he said pointing to a framed portrait on the wall.

We beheld the late Richard Corkright. The gentleman was a bit unusual in appearance, stout and red-haired with a steely gaze that belied his somewhat comical appearance.

"What can you tell us about your late employer?"

"Exactly what I told the police, sir. He was a kind, sober, pious man was Mr. Corkright. Not overly pleasant company, to be candid. Nor given to the idle courtesies of many gentlemen of his rank, but hard working, diligent, honest as the day is long."

"What happened on the fateful day?"

"Well, sir, I came to the office, as usual, at fifteen before the hour. My employer arrived at his usual time: the hour itself."

"The hour being…"

"Eight o'clock, sir."

"Anything out of the ordinary that day?"

"The day started in a very typical manner. Mr. Corkright came in his usual fashion and acted his usual stoic self, content to go into his office with no more greeting than reciting my name. That morning I had to stop him. You see, he had not been in the office since the early afternoon of the previous day, a court appearance occupying his time until our closing, and he had missed the afternoon post. A letter had arrived, and I gave it to him."

"What can you tell us about that letter, Mr. De Greek?" interrupted Holmes.

"It bore a continental postmark. The address was unfamiliar and there was no name."

"Did Mr. Corkright show any emotion at receiving it?

"Yes, sir, you could say so. He looked rather troubled. I asked him if he was alright, but got no reply. Carried the letter like he knew it to be ill-omened. Went straight into his office and shut his door tight. That was the last time I ever saw him."

"Anything else of consequence happen that morning? Anything at all out of the ordinary?"

"Nothing related to Mr. Cockright. There was a peculiar incident. I don't know why it sticks out in my mind except that I can't recall anything like it ever happening before in this quiet little neighborhood of ours. A loud fight somehow broke out on the steps of the office."

"And how did you handle the situation?"

"Well, sir, when I heard the commotion I rose from my desk and ran to the entrance to see what was the source of the awful den. I threw open the door and saw there two young gentlemen in a physical altercation of some sort. I stepped between them. Each tried to plead his case to me – something about a tavern bill - but I had none of it. I sent the two scrappers on their way. That sort of thing can't be tolerated in a decent neighborhood."

"Approximately what time did this incident occur?"

"I'd say around eight thirty."

"Exactly how long were you away from your desk?"

"Not more than two minutes I am sure."

Holmes nodded, changed the subject abruptly.

"I take it this is the only entrance to the establishment."

"The one and only, sir."

"And would you be so kind as to show us the office."

The gentleman nodded gravely, and retrieving a key from his pocket, opened the door communicating with the dead man's office. Pitch black was the space before us. and cold and musty, with an aura of morbidity and decay.

"Begging you pardon, gentlemen, let me turn on the gaslights."

Two gas lamps were lighted and the office cam into dim view. We entered. The scene before us was rather crude, though still a tidy arrangement, clearly designed for function more than comfort. The room was, or at least seemed, a bit broader than the lobby we had just left, with a noticeably lower ceiling. There was a desk and a chair. The walls to the left and right contained simple woodwork. The back wall stood out, as it was quite incongruous with the simple décor of the rest of the room. It was brightly plastered from top to bottom, containing in its midsection a baroque fireplace, with a red marble mantel and attached half-columns.

I groaned. "A windowless room. You couldn't pay me enough to labor in a place like this."

"I know just what you mean, Mr. Watson," responded the secretary in a charming lisp. "But it is sufficiently ventilated. Lack of windows makes a room more secure. A lawyer's office has many objects of value and one can never be too careful."

"True, Mr. De Greek-"

"A magnificent fireplace, wouldn't you say, Watson?"

I studied it for a brief moment.

"Oh, yes. I noticed it when we entered, Holmes. Gorgeous marble mantle."

Mr. De Greek seemed to take a measure of satisfaction in our praise. "Do you think so, sir? It's fine enough, but not quite what Mr. Corkright asked for when it was remodeled."

"When was it remodeled?"

"Oh, about six months ago roughly. By the son of a friend. The young man's first commission I believe it was. I fear he was a bit overzealous."

"Why was the wall remodeled?"

"It certainly wasn't in need of any renovation. It was mostly done as, shall we say, a favor to the young man."

Holmes took out his magnifying glass, began inspecting back wall, then turned his attention to the floor.

"Mr. De Greek, the paper gives an account of what happened that day. But would you kindly tell Dr. Watson and myself, in your own words, what exactly you found upon entering this room?"

He responded with exceeding gravity. "I opened the room with my key and saw the poor fellow laying there in the center of the floor. The place was a mess, the room showered with papers, the desk was all upset. I straightened up a bit after the police were finished with their investigation. I'm not sure why the idea came into my fool-head. A tidy office isn't much good to a dead man."

"You did you duty, sir," said I.

The man raised his chin in acknowledgment. "One certainly tries to, Mr. Watson."

My friend, having finished his examination put away his magnifying glass. He pointed in a certain direction

"And there, I take it, is the safe whose contents were robbed?"

"Yes, sir."

"Was it usually locked?"

"Yes, sir. Always. And only my employer had the combination and the key necessary to access it."

"Just the two of you in the office on that day?"

"Quite correct. Just the two of us."

"No visitors. No clients that day?"

"No, sir, none. One was expected that afternoon. Visitors are sparse on Fridays."

Holmes took hold of the bell-rope in the corner, gave a yank. A sound reverberated in the lobby.

"Seems to be in working order." He noted to himself.

"Quite, sir."

My companion wondered silently about the room, examining both floor and walls. At one point he paced from one end of the room to the other. Our patient guide waited, then, after perhaps two or three full minutes, asked if there anything else he could assist us with. Holmes responded with a dubious sigh.

"Not at present, Mr. De Greek. We will detain you no longer. Thank you for your assistance."

He indicated that it had been a pleasure. The kind man turned off the gas lights and escorted us to the door in true servant fashion. He took a final look about the place, indulging in one fleeting moment of nostalgia, then drew to a close the door to the office, and, I suppose, to a long chapter of his life. He graciously dismissed our final expressions of gratitude, wishing us every success in our investigation, then walked away in the dignified gait of a humble servant.

Chapter 3

A Hidden Way

I assumed our preliminary investigation to be concluded, and was thus quite surprised to find my companion walking, without comment, around the street corner and into the alley by which we came. There, he silently conducted an investigation as I leaned upon my umbrella. Empty crates lay about and Holmes moved them, studying the wall and floor area they had covered. I thought the old boy was clutching at straws, but knew better than to interrupt. Seeking to pleasantly pass the time, took to humming a tune from Tchaikovsky's "The Queen of Spades", an aria from Act III, I believe.

Holmes stepped away from the wall and came to stand beside me, signifying that his examination had concluded.

"Ah, I am afraid that life is not a game, murder investigation least of all," commented he drolly,

"Very good. Well, Holmes?"

"Well, Watson, you know my methods. Do you see anything noteworthy in this place?"

I looked about as I answered.

"It seems indistinguishable from every other alley I've encountered in my time."

These simple words managed to grate upon my friend. "Truly you educate me on the subject, sir. I was not aware that it was common for alleys in the Queen's London to possess scrapings marks likes these here running nearly the width of the alley in perfect symmetry. I am further enlightened to learn that all alleys in this fair city are graced with inexplicable two-foot deep holes like that one far against the wall over there."

At his smug tone I took offense. I became defiant.

"Come, Holmes, all places have their random, idiomatic features. Probably tied to the remodeling done here six months ago. What possible significance could they have?"

"These anomalies (and they are anomalies, my dear Watson) occur in one location, and that location is directly behind the murder scene. It lies beyond the boundaries of coincidence. These are things worthy of pondering. We deal with a clever criminal, and it is upon a few such clues that our case must be advanced. Especially that hole there on the edge. Its existence seems to me wholly inexplicable. Yet I am convinced that the thing was made in a particular place for a particular purpose. To a person of superior observatory skills it sticks out like an elephant's trunk would on a lady."

I maintained my wounded disposition. Holding my umbrella rather like a hammer, I began banging the handle against the brick surface of the wall.

"I say, Watson, to what purpose do you thoughtlessly abuse your personal effects?"

"I am no fool, Holmes. You have implied a secret entrance. I am scrutinizing your theory. I see no gaps in the mortar, nor do I detect any hollow passage behind them."

My companion shrugged.

"And yet I'd stake my life on this being the means of entry and escape for our killer. All signs point to an entrance in this vicinity. A very well concealed entrance. Oh, well. Let us be off."

And I followed, dumbfounded as to the exact status of our investigation.

***

We returned to McGeady Street and shortly found a taxi stand. For the first leg of the ride back to Baker Street we were silent, for Holmes was deep in thought and I hesitated to interrupt. I, however, found the silence vexing and eventually made an attempt to converse with my preoccupied friend.

"The murderer I assume to have been hiding in the office when ole Corkright came in."

"Naturally, Watson. Else the man would have had time to ring the bell-rope and summoned aid."

"I hate to say it, Holmes, but can we rule out some sort of 'inside job'? As charming as that gentleman Mr. De Greek was, he is the only witness to events that morning before the police were summoned. Could he not have simply carried out the crime?"

"That gentleman with the puny frame strangle a large, healthy man the size of our victim? Highly unlikely. Could he have let the murder in and out? Possibly, but my intuition warns against such a simple resolution. Assuming the secretary has told the police and us the exhaustive truth (and we have no reason to believe that he hasn't) we have the puzzling scenario of a man murdered inside a small, windowless room with a ventilation system that would not afford entrance or exit to even the smallest of men."

"A small child or a midget of some sort might be accommodated," I pointed out, helpfully.

"Again you overlook the obvious: the stature of our victim. Did a small child or a man of 'midget' stature brutally throttle a grown man? No, Watson, that won't do."

"Perhaps the killer hid in the office after committing his crime and then snuck around old De Greek when he entered into the room? He would have been, after all, distracted by the sight of his dead employer. I saw something like that in play once."

My friend scoffed. "And I've seen it in a dozen plays, Watson, and I tell you such a thing is highly unlikely, even factoring in the carelessness of an abstracted mind. A thorough inspection was conducted, so it is equally unlikely that our killer remained behind to exit after the police departed the scene. No, no, a secret door is the only logical means of ingress or escape. All signs point to a hidden entrance communicating from the office to the alley."

"The paper said that the police searched thoroughly for one. As did we."

"Which means only that it is cleverly concealed. But what can be hidden by one man can be unearthed by another."

"I say, Holmes, there's something that been troubling me."

"And what is that, Watson?"

"Corkright appears to have opened the safe for the intruder. Why would a thief kill a man after that, after he's cooperated with him?"

My companion leaned back, locked his fingers together in his lap; "An excellent point, Watson. Let us assume for the sake of argument that the thievery took place immediately upon Corkright entering his office just after eight o'clock, as I am quite certain it did. Corkright, under threat of violence, was made to quietly unlock the safe, yes? The thief divested it of its valuable contents, estimated to be between ten and twenty thousand pounds. All this is clear and rational. But, as you rightly point out, there is nothing to be gained by killing a defenseless man at that point. Why not bound and gag the old duffer and quietly quit the room, knowing you have hours before he will be discovered – ample time in which to make an escape? Wiser still, why not close the safe door, take the esteemed solicitor with you, and make the police think the crooked lawyer has taken the funds and precious items entrusted to him and flown the coop like a shady character in some dime-store romance? You could drop your hostage off in some remote location as you flee the country. By the time the truth is fully uncovered, you could be contently sipping your port in Cape Town or Macau or La Serena."

"Wouldn't it be better to eliminate the hostage once his usefulness is at an end?"I noted, feeling somewhat clever at correcting Holmes' theory. My friend responded with a short laugh.

"Watson! Now you're thinking like a criminal – a very dumb criminal I'm afraid. Miscreants of even modest intelligence always allow for the possibility of arrest. Why risk a trip to the hangman with an unnecessary murder? But we stray from our task with such idle speculations. The fact is that a defenseless man was strangled, seemingly unnecessarily."

"Very perplexing, Holmes."

"Indeed, Watson, for the moment."

"Well, I can't think on an empty stomach. What say I have Mrs. Hudson bring us an early supper?"

"Do what you must. Contemplating this matter will involve my full attention, and I have no appetite at the moment. Foul deeds have been done, Watson, and I am certain more are to come."

Upon our return to our apartment, I ate a hearty supper as Holmes smoked his pipes and fondled a brick he had carried with him from the alley. The evening edition of paper arrived just as I finished my custard, and we silently read it. As I prepared to retire that night, I left my companion reading a book on the subject quite possibly fartherest removed from our present case: the statuary of antiquity.

Chapter 4

A New Victim

Tuesday dawn commenced at its accustomed hour. I awoke to find a smiling Sherlock Holmes hovering over me, seemingly in exceptionally good spirits. In his hands he held a length of rope and a rounded metallic pole.

"Sorry to wake you, old boy," he said. "I've had a most productive morning! And I may have a workable theory on the Merton case. But I will need some assistance. Are you game?"

As it happened I had no patients scheduled that morning and knew a nearby colleague of mine would be keeping office hours. Thus, I was free to assist. Wiping the sleep from my eyes, I left my warm bed and made ready.

***

Our route back to Merton the next day was not direct. We stopped at a blacksmith's establishment, tucked away off of Benbow Street, where Holmes picked up an object wrapped in a towel (an order having been relayed by errand boy earlier that morning). Holmes discretely inspected the object without comment, then, apparently finding it satisfactory, paid the bill, and we left. Upon our return to the alley behind the murdered lawyer's office, Holmes placed the pole he had brought in the hole at the far side of the alleyway. He then walked over to the wall of the building containing the murder room and proceeded to examine it with a piercing glance. I followed suit. It was comprised of rather commonplace black and red bricks, many of which were pocked with small indentations. Try though I might, I saw nothing out of the ordinary. My companion spoke.

"We have already firmly ruled out the murderer climbing through the chimney. And yet, I am convinced that it was indeed the chimney that provided an entrance."

"What makes you think so?"

"External and internal observation, Watson. Externally, we note these peculiar scrapping marks stretching from the wall here (corresponding to the chimney's right side) to the artificial hole on the far end of the alley. This surely accounts for a door of some kind."

"And internally?"

"During our visit to the office yesterday, I observed an abundance of particles of debris concentrated on the fireplace's immediate right side. Our killer was apparently rude enough to refrain from wiping his feet before entering the premises. These two observations tell me the location of the secret entrance. But how to operate it! I pondered the matter, Watson, long into the night and almost gave up, when suddenly the scheme of the whole thing hit me.

"And what might that be?"

"I shall show you shortly. For the present, observe these bricks." He pointed to the wall.

"Straight column formation. Black and red. A common enough pattern."

"Did you notice that the bricks on either side of the remodeled area are laid in the overlapping format? "

"I suppose I did."

"And did you note the abundance of dimples?"

"That I did also note. A shoddy variety, it would seem."

"Shoddy, if the purchaser was strictly concerned with quality of bricks. Not shoddy if that person was interested in concealing something. I draw your attention to this one in particular, Watson."

He indicated a notch in a black brick located toward the bottom section of the wall. Kneeling down and examining it, I found it to contain in its center a deep indentation.

"Indeed, this is unnatural and surely manmade, Holmes," I conceded. "But not quite wide enough for an entrance." I indulged in a laugh.

My friend remained stoic. "On the contrary, Watson, it is wide enough to allow entrance, not of a person, but rather a device such as this."

Here he unwrapped the towel to reveal large metallic item loosely in the shape of a thin, oversized key with a ring on the end. He gingerly placed the device in the hole and pushed it approximately half its length, then slowly turned it ninety degrees clockwise. This movement ended in the distinct sound of a click from within the wall, at which Holmes let out a small cry of triumph. Still not sure of its significance, I witnessed Holmes attach one end of the rope we had brought with us to the ring-end of the key, then walk to the other end of the alley and wrap the other end of the rope around the pole he had placed in the hole. He pulled it taunt.

"A relief my prototype worked! I feared we might have to modify it repeatedly until a functional design was found. Obviously not a very sophisticated device, else a more exact fit would have been required. You appreciate the situation, Watson?"

I studied the display, put into motion my scrapheap of a brain.

"I believe so. A crude locking device has been installed. Unlocked, a section of the wall can be pulled out by this equally crude pulley system. But how Holmes? The bricks are plastered together."

"So it appears, Watson. So it appears."

"And we haven't so much as a chisel."

"I think this will serve our purposes much better."

Here Holmes produced a small touch and tinderbox.

"Holmes, you're mad!"

I thought his intention was to attempt to burn through solid brick. He laughed at my incredible naivety.

"Mad, Watson? Observe!"

My friend lit his torch and placed the flame near the bricks around keyhole. To my amazement, the mortar seemed to slowly dissolve. Thus was revealed a square configuration of bricks detached from the rest of the wall, at the exact center of which sat the brick with the keyhole.

"Amazing!" said I, spellbound as I watched the mortar melt away.

"You've studied the artistry of antiquity, Watson? Do you know how cracks in marble statues were corrected during the glory of Greece and Rome? Marble dust and wax were mixed together and used to seal them. It was temporal deception, but effective. Now, how do you suppose our engineer concealed the cracks about his secret door?"

"Dried mortar and wax!"

"Very good, Watson. Or perhaps simply ground quartz and wax. A solution quick drying and to the naked eye – and even to the amplified one – virtually indistinguishable from regular mortar. Now, if you would be so kind to step over here."

He motioned for me to take the end section of the rope in his hand. I did so.

"The block is unfastened. I am sure it is partially hollowed out and that there are rollers of some kind on the bottom. Still, it will not be overly light. I know how unaccustomed to manual labor you are, doctor, and this may be a bit of strain. Please indulge me, sir, and pull!

With some effort, we pulled and were rewarded when a section of wall came loose, a block corresponding, it suddenly dawned on me, to the size of one of the oversized pedestals under one of the fireplace's half-pillar. We continued to pull and brought the section of wall to cover roughly three-quarters of the narrow alley way.

My companion let go of the rope. He clapped his hands loudly in triumph. "Good enough, Watson! Good enough. We've made our point. We know how the killer entered and escaped. This block can be brought entirely out of the wall, taking almost the entire width of the alley, and pushed over, creating an entrance. The design is crude but effective, allowing for quick removal and restoration."

I was panting. "Holmes, I don't believe it. It must have been placed there during the renovation."

"Of that I'm entirely sure, Watson."

"But is it truly large enough for a large man to make use of?"

"Just big enough, I should say. With not an inch to spare!"

"The killer had assistance, I take it?"

"At least four, I assume."

I nodded. "Four men could remove it quickly enough."

"Two strapping lads, I am sure, were sufficient to efficiently operate it."

"Then what were the other two for?"

"That will be made clear in time, Watson."

I dismissed the issue for the moment. "A brilliant scheme, Holmes. But to do it on a workday. Didn't the perpetrators risk witnesses?"

"We've just done it on a Tuesday morning, old bean, and what witnesses do you account for? This far end of "High Street" is a rather secluded area. The perpetrators likely passed off as workmen in order to draw as little attention as possible."

"But listen to that grating noise we made as we dragged it across the pavement. How was it not heard from within?"

"You are referring, of course, to Mr. De Greek. The scuffle on the doorstep Friday morning would have served as a workable distraction. It gave our murderer and his accomplices perhaps two full minutes to remove the block, let the killer escape, then restore it. A quick patch job around the block's borders, and their task was complete."

I beamed a smile. "Things are shaping up nicely. Only our second day on the case and we already have our criminal."

"We have an entrance, Watson," Holmes corrected me. "Let us be content with that for the moment. We must not get ahead of established facts."

At this I started. So great was my agitation that my words almost choked in my mouth.

"Comes, Holmes. Is it possible the architect who put this chimney in six month ago was ignorant of this entrance."

"It is not inconceivable, Watson. Did the good secretary not say that the architect was young and inexperienced? If he were wanting in vigilance, some other party may have put it in under his nose. Time will resolve that riddle. In the meantime, I say we keep it our little secret."

"You don't intend to withhold this from the police, Holmes?"

"Only temporarily, Watson. They would likely overweigh its significance, just as you have, my old friend. Come, give me a hand."

With some effort, we restored the section of the wall. To discourage any snooping, a few empty crates were placed before the location of the secret entrance. We made our way around the corner to the street.

"I'd say an interview with the architect who restored the office is in order," I suggested emphatically.

"As would I, Watson. In due time."

"I should think the sooner the better," I persisted.

Before Holmes could respond, however, our attention was diverted by the sound of a shrill voice calling in our direction. A winded policeman came up to us.

"Mr. Holmes! Thank goodness. Your landlady said you'd be here."

"What is it, my good man?"

"Inspector McVay requests you come right away, sir, to this location."

The man handed Holmes a piece of paper.

Holmes read it in a glance. "Lower Havering? What is the urgency?"

"There's been another of 'em tarot murders, sir!"

***

Arriving at Lower Havering with dispatch, and venturing down the indicated steep path that lay on the outskirts of an old suburb, we came to a remote pond. There we beheld the fifth victim of the tarot card killer. He was a large fellow, with shoulders like an ox and hands the size of frying pans. Il Cinque di Coope from the now infamous Italian deck was pinned to his face. Holmes immediately took to examining the cup found near the corpse.

Inspector McVay spoke. "Received an anonymous tip we did a few hours ago. A queer note in some fancy writing. Said to look by this here pond."

Holmes was occupied in smelling the cup. "A lingering bouquet of grapes...plum...figs... chocolate." He paused to take a deep snort. "Something else. Very subtle. Just a hint of something metallic. The King of Poisons, I'd wager."

"Fanciful dessert!" noted I in macabre fashion.

"Italian red wine, Watson. Rosso di Montalicino, I believe. Mixed with arsenic-laced sawdust, unless I miss my guess. Nice to see that our killer is evolving toward more sophisticated methods."

At this McVay frowned. "Ain't nothing to joke about, Mr. Holmes. We have a maniac on our hands."

"Perhaps," responded Holmes. "Or perhaps someone merely imitating one."

The inspector gave a defiant growl. "Imitation or real article, I'll find the scoundrel. And see him hanged for his crimes! I would ask you to delay your investigation into the other case until this matter is resolved."

"The other case, Inspector?"

"The Corkright job, Mr. Holmes. This tarot card fellow is a threat to public safety and must be accorded the highest priority."

"A threat to public safety?" responded Holmes. "Of that I'm not convinced. Nor that these murders and the untimely demise of Mr. Richard Corkright are unrelated."

The inspector laughed at such a notion."Begging your pardon, Mr. Holmes, what possible connection could there be between robbery in an upscale neighborhood and maniacal murder in the slums?"

The Inspector's levity served only to make my companion all the graver.

"Different crimes in different areas, Inspector," he noted quietly. "And yet these bizarre cases initiated within one day of each other. When you've held your post a bit longer, you'll learn to be suspicious of such a coincidence."

"Any idea who this poor bloke is, Inspector?" I asked.

"Aye, Dr. Watson, a pretty lass wandered in here not an hour ago, claiming she was his girl. James Purvey is his name. She last saw him this morning. Been acting funny last week, according to her. She was quite hysterical, so I had Peyser escort her home."

"May I speak with her?"

"By all means, Mr. Holmes, if you like. I took down her address. Here." He tore a leaf from his notebook and handed it to Holmes. "She lives near here with her mother. But I should tell you that I'm convinced of her innocence."

"I'm no less convinced of it, Inspector. But it may give us a fresh track down which to explore. Come, Watson."

And so we, address in hand, trudged up the incline back to the road.

***

Holmes and I found, with little inconvenience or delay, the residence of Miss Molly Sounders, the young lady in question. The girl was strong, slender, and feeble. Presently, she sat before us, comforted by her dutiful mother, a plump lady of at least fifty. Even in her grief, the young woman was as pretty as a rosebud – perhaps all the more so for it. She addressed us, in a tone somber and sweet, with eyes full of great sorrow

"Oh, it still doesn't seem real. Like some terrible dream. My cousin Jenny and I were returning from the Tilbury Street station (where we sell apple pastries to make a bit). We was walking along, carrying out basket between us like we always does, laughing and singing, and we stop all of sudden 'cause we sees the police at the edge of the road."

She stopped.

"Go on," Holmes coaxed.

"He loved to sit down there by the pond in the cool shadows, for he was a rather solitary fellow at times. So I has this feeling I has and I thought right away that it was him. I let go of the basket and ran down there and a copper grabs me and says 'You don't want to go there, Miss, unless you want to see a dead man... " And the poor creature fell to sobbing.

"Strength, my love," consoled the mother. "That behemoth of yours has gone to a better place."

Holmes spoke. "I know it's difficult, Miss Sounders, but please try to compose yourself. Your assistance is badly needed. Others have fallen to the same fate as your paramour, and unless action is taken, more may yet fall victim. Now, please tell us what you can about James Purvey. What did he do for a living?"

"He didn't make a living," bolted the mother.

"Oh, mama, what a thing to say! He surely did work. He got by on odd jobs."

"Odd jobs?"

"This and that."

"Legal sorts of jobs?"

"Legal sorts of job! Hem! That bear of man in legal work!" said the mother.

"Mother, please! Mr. Holmes, what Jimmy did was not illegal, not as such. Mostly he was involved in..."

"Go on."

"Dog fighting, Mr. Holmes, which ain't strictly speaking against the law. Oh, I know it's a brutal thing to have them poochies fight and tear into each other and for men to drink and laugh and bet on 'em and the like, but he says – he used to say, that is - them creatures is made for fighting and nothing else, like gamecocks, and how he had to do the dirty sorts of work because he'd never been given an education or hand up to learn a proper trade."

"Ghastly trade, if you ask me," said the old lady.

It was I who answered her. "Oh, I entirely agree, madam. The full weight of the law should be brought down-"

Holmes cut me off. "Be that as it may, Watson, were not here to determine the moral merits of the industry. Come, Miss Sounders, tell me who were his colleagues in these events?"

"Well, there was a Caputo, who he paled around with. A bloke named Jaggers (who they called Jags) sometimes sold him dogs, warned him of police raids and the like.

There was a Jewison, whom they called "Rabbi", though I'm sure he weren't one. Some fancy gent made most of the arrangements. I only met him a few times."

"And what was his name?"

"Why, I can't rightly recall. We were never introduced proper like. Jimmie called him Stewie now that I think of it."

Holmes asked: "Might the name have been Stewart Nuss?"

A light shone briefly in her watery eyes. "Oh, yes, that's it! I remember him mentioning it once. Nuss was the feller's name."

The name rang a bell in my dim-witted brain. Then I recalled it as belonging to the nephew of the late Richard Corkright.

"Tell me, did he mention any Gumbell?"

The name had no meaning for me.

"No, I don't believe so," answered the girl.

"How about MacBride?"

Nor did that name have any relevance. Then I understood Holmes game.

"No, not in my presence," answered the young lady to the name Holmes had just offered.

"No Mercier? Meyer? Newlan, Newquist?"

"Wait! Yes, the last one, Dirk Newquist I think."

"What of Dirk Newquist?"

"He and his brother had dogs they owned and trained. They used to be actors but somehow got drummed out of that line of work. Loud and nasty they were, always leering at me. You know the type." She began crying again. "Oh, but, Mr. Holmes, don't think poor of my man. He may have associated with a questionable sort of men, but he was good to me, always wanted the best for me. Told me we'd live in nice house in the country someday away from the foul-smelling city air and how I wouldn't have to ever worry again."

The young woman made a gesture of anguish and despair, then buried her face in her mother's waiting bosom.

"There, my child, there!"

I spoke up. "Holmes, perhaps we can resume this discussion at another time. Miss Molly, I fear, has had a frightful day."

The mother responded. "Thank you, sir! You're good to my child! A frightful day it's been for us both."

Holmes rose from his seat. "One final question, then, Miss Sounders. Where did James Purvey live?"

"In a small rented room not far from here. With his two cousins."

"Would you know their names?"

"Dornbeck was their name. Larry and Bob. Oh, they'll be torn down when they hears of this! Oh, who's to tell them? They were close as brothers!"

Dornbeck! Again, a name steeped in tragedy!

"That's for the police to worry about, my dear," I said soothingly. "You must try to get some rest. And have faith. Eternal wisdom hath its ends, my child."

"It surely does, sir," agreed the mother.

I am not what you would call a religious man, but I am willing to utilize what resource of comfort lay at my disposal.

"Dr. Watson is quite right. Do try to rest. We'll be leaving now."

The young woman's eyes were wide in terror. "Rest? How am I to get rest? I be afraid to step outside my door."

Holmes was smiling comfortingly. "I assure you, my dear, you're perfectly safe. You and your mother."

"Quite safe," I affirmed, feigning agreement with my companion, though I could not see the basis for his affirmation.

"Oh, are you sure, sir?" persisted the young lady, hopefully.

"Entirely, Miss Sounders. The case will be resolved before a week has elapsed."

And taking the poor creature's hand each, we bid her goodbye. It seemed she was starting to mend, her violent sadness beginning to give way to calm despair.

Chapter 5

A Trip to Bexley

We left the house of mourning and began walking down the street. I immediately took to shaking my head.

"How could she not know her lover's cousins were found murdered three days ago?" I pondered aloud.

Holmes shrugged somberly. "She's obviously illiterate, only knows what others tell her. Somehow the news has escaped her."

"Queer Purvey didn't mention it to her," I noted. My friend nodded his head gravely.

"Very queer. A man's two beloved cousins are brutally murdered, and he fails to tell his lover. Days later he has a clandestine meeting with the killer, during which he himself is poisoned. Yes, very queer, Watson. I fear it all portends no good."

"It seems so shadowy to me," I said.

Holmes nodded slowly.

"Yes, Watson, to me as well. But where there is shadow there must also be light. Let us work toward the light and all shall me illuminated. Young Mr. Nuss, nephew to the late Richard Corkright, stands at the crossroads between these two cases of ours. To his home let us off!"

I decided to change the subject, prompted by a low growling in my stomach.

"I do hate to bring it up, Holmes, but I feel I must point out that it's well past noontide and I haven't eaten since breakfast."

"Time is a precious commodity, my friend. Can't you wait a bit, old boy?"

"Of course I could, but I for one work better on a full stomach. It occurs to me that there's a place not far from here. Ole Chidester's eating house. It used to be over on Taylop Street, not a quarter of an hour from here."

My friend sighed. "Then by all means let us make peace between you and your rumbling belly, but with sufficient alacrity. Afterwards, we can have a meeting with the begrieved Mr. Stewart Nuss."

We found the place easily enough, exactly where I remembered it being. I settled to my repast with enthusiasm, the fare being an excellent serving of boiled beef and cabbage stew seasoned with stone pine. My companion contented himself with black tea and his comfy pipe. I noted a dark brooding in his eyes. I hardly finished the last morsel before my friend rose and began making his way toward the door, leaving me but time to settle my account and fly in his direction.

**

The papers had reported Stewart Nuss as residing in Christchurch, the very heart of Bexley, an area with which I had some familiarity. We accomplished the distance between the excellent eating house on Taylop Street and that borough in tolerable time, arriving in good season, the only complication being negotiating the Erith Marsh. From the local constabulary we obtained the address of Mr. Nuss, and finding it to be nearby, we set out on foot.

Not twenty minutes later, we stood on the threshold of the young man's rude domicile. The young gentleman answered the door. He was tall and lanky, with a deep tan. We introduced ourselves, giving our names and the purpose of the visit. Nuss scrutinized us with what I though a rather haughty gaze, then reluctantly gave us entry. I took an instant dislike to the fellow, for he had a wicked and eager aspect about him. A sunburned face on an honest workman has a noble bearing, but on dandies and ne'er-do-wells it takes on a more distasteful hue. He took us back into a meager parlor where he bent low before us in a bow I took for mockery, but which my generous companion treated as the best style of courtesy, returning the salute in kind. He addressed us in a familiar fashion.

"Welcome to my humble home, gentlemen. What service can I bring?"

It was Holmes that answered.

"First, allow me and Dr. Watson to offer our condolences. We are sorry to intrude in your hour of grief."

Nuss smiled the smile of a Jackal. "I appreciate that and all, but truly what's to be sorry about, sir? We all got to die some day. You, me, the doctor here. My uncle just found his way out of the world a bit early is all, with help I grant you. But it's a trek we must all take."

"Your sentiment is valid, even if the words are crude. May I ask what it is you do for a living, Mr. Nuss?"

He seemed somehow pleased at the question. "Entertainment is my business, Mr. Holmes. Public entertainment. Now, I'm sure fine gentlemen such as yourselves have no need for it, the theatre and opera houses and what not being available to you. But to those inhabiting, shall we say, a station a bit lower than yours, more vulgar pleasures are highly prized and there's good money to be made in providing them -."

"You are entitled to any vocation and philosophy you like, Mr. Nuss," my companion interrupted with his usual impatience. "My companion and I are here in an official capacity and only interested in specific facts. Can you tell me how you found out of your Uncle's untimely demise?"

The young man seated himself, but offered none to his guests.

"Word didn't reach me too quickly. I was out of town when the whole thing happened."

"Where were you?"

"If it's any business of yours, I was at a swimming gala in East Lindley over in Lincolnshire with friends. Such things, I believe, being perfectly legal."

As this conversation ensued, I made note of Nuss' collection of strange talismans and worry beads on a nearby table. Truly an odd character in both word and deed!

"How long were you in Lincolnshire?" asked Holmes.

"The whole weekend. I left last Thursday afternoon with three friends. I came home yesterday morning and found a policeman waiting on my doorstep. Was he as told me."

"Were you and your uncle close, Mr. Nuss?"

He squirmed a bit, then settled into his chair like a heathen sultan. "That's a personal question, Mr. Holmes. But to answer it directly, no, we were not on what you might call friendly terms."

It was now Holmes who began snooping around the room as he continued to question the young man.

The young man continued. "I'm an orphan, Mr. Holmes. My uncle was my only kin and I was his. But he never did take to me. He loaned me a bit now and then, but it always came with a quarrel. He swore he did me favors only for my dead mother's sake. To be clear, I always paid him back. I even offered a percentage to him, which he pridefully refused it. Now, why make a lad down on his luck feel bad if he's willing to give you a percentage for your trouble? That the kind of hard man he was. And it weren't like he didn't have plenty! But as he's left the world, I'll speak no further ill of him."

"You're his heir in all things, are you?" I asked, trying to be helpful.

"As I just said, Doctor, I'm his only family."

"And when do you take the estate?" queried Holmes.

"I spoke with my uncle's solicitor this very morning. He tells me the will-reading will be Monday next."

"Would you mind telling me your solicitor's name?"

"Why should I mind? It's Mr. Arwin Romanus over in Camden. Here." And here he handed Holmes a card.

"Thank you kindly," said my friend putting the card away. "A bit of an imposition making a young man wait so long for his much-deserved inheritance."

The young man laughed, and it was a nasty sort of rumble, a rolling growl belonging more to the race of crocodiles than man. "Well, I got by this long without it! What's a few more days?"

"The public entertainment industry keeps you well enough, does it?"

"Well enough, for now. But I got ambitions."

The young man seemed to remember his manners, now offering us each a seat. We were presented silver-ringed cigarettes from a case, I declining, Holmes accommodating.

"Ambitions you say?" asked my friend after lighting his fag and expelling smoke from nostrils and mouth.

"Aye, I do. What's a young fellow without dream?"

"For instance?"

"I don't see what it has to do with your gentlemen's investigation, but a recently acquired friend of mine is putting together a worldwide carnival company over on the mainland. He's got all the know-how, friends in right places and the like. He just needs some capital to make the whole thing come about. Now, I'll be able to be his partner. When we're household names, you'll be able to say you knew me when I was a just poor, hustling lad."

"I will, no doubt, recollect the gracious privilege afforded me. And should I care to one day pen a biography, what shall I say was Mr. Stewart Nuss' line of work before finding his success in the entertainment industry?"

"I like you, Mr. Holmes!" There was a grin running the full length of his mouth.

Holmes nodded.

"I did odd jobs. I worked for my uncle off and on again. He and that snooty secretary of his helped me find employment once or twice."

"Odd jobs would no doubt account for such an interesting assortment there," said Holmes, gesturing toward a table full of tools.

"I gets a tool, I keeps it. Never know when a tool will come in handy."

Holmes and Nuss left their seats and went over to the table.

"Your collection of files is most impressive, Mr. Stewart. It may interest you to know that I have written three monographs on files. May I?"

"Please."

Holmes picked up a file, examined it closely. "Marvelous construction. Light, durable. The teeth seem a bit dull."

"You can trust me, it'll get the job done."

"May I ask where you came by this fine collection of files?"

"De Greek. That secretary to my late uncle. (You probably met the blighter already). He tried to get me into locksmithing sometime back."

"Did he?"

"Oh, yes. He was one as a young man, back before he became a fancy desk clerk. Now, I think I'll have a drink. Can I offer you gentlemen something? I guess I let my manners slip."

"No, thank you kindly, Mr. Nuss," said Holmes rising. I rose as well. "We've taken up enough of your time. Best of luck in all your endeavors. Come, Watson, let us bother Mr. Nuss no more…"

And we left with nods but not another word exchanged.

"What do you think of our boy there, Watson?" asked Holmes on the street. I took to shaking my head in a confounded fashion.

"Oh, I can readily think of a dozen men more worthy of inheriting a small fortune. There is little remarkable about him. Just another undeserving recipient of Lady Fortune's favor. And he didn't seem terribly concerned with his uncle's passing."

"No, he didn't. But the law does not convict men for their feelings, only their actions."

"It was he who stood the most to gain from Richard Corkright's passing," I pointed out.

"A fact, I am sure, that has not escaped the notice of the police, Watson. But if his alibi holds, and I suspect it will, he should have no reason to fear the law," returned Holmes, with emphasis on the last two words.

"I assume our next visit will be with the architect?"

Holmes found my persistence amusing. "Patience, Watson. It's been an eventful day. Your long anticipated encounter with the novice architect shall take place tomorrow, post meridian!"

Chapter 6

Three Friends

Next day, Wednesday, came bright and cheerful, and I obeyed my usual weekday routine of rising with the first light of the sun. Over breakfast, Holmes announced to me his intention to briefly suspend his investigation into both the Tarot murders and the Merton murder case, as he planned to spend the bulk of the morning on an unrelated errand (done at the behest of a coffee importer in Ilford to whom he owed a favor). He, however, had every intention of resuming our present cases that afternoon with a visit first to Mr. Romanus of Camden, the solicitor of the late Richard Corkiright, and secondly to the young architect by the name of Phillip Wakeham. I found my afternoon schedule clear and, made plain my desire to accompany Holmes on his journey, I agreed to close shop early and return home, thus enabling as to depart for Camden together.

My abridged day of work came and went, and with its conclusion I locked my cheerless green door and quickly bent my steps toward Baker's street. Annoyed at the congestion, I traded one boulevard for another, but to little avail. Fearful of missing Holmes, I decided to achieve my destination by a route less direct but more open, and turned down a familiar alleyway.

Lost in thought, I suddenly became aware of footsteps to my rear. Next thing I knew, I stood crouched over, having made, in the wink of an eye, a sudden duck, driven by an overpowering instinctive impulse. A loud thumping sound resounded behind me. Looking in that direction, I, with calm horror, witnessed a quivering object in the wooden planking on the wall behind me. I gaped about, but saw no suspicious party.

Two or three good Samaritans rushed into the alley (I had apparently screamed, though I have no distinct recollection of having done so), offering what assistance they could. I fear I showed no proper gratitude, my mind completely preoccupied in its attempt to grasp the situation that had just unfolded. Largely ignoring my would-be benefactors, I walked to the wall on which the missile hung, and retrieved it. In my hand I held a short spear of some kind, the shaft of which was, I would estimate, to have been roughly one and a half meters. I took the weapon with which I had been assaulted and, bearing it under my arm, made my way home along the path of my original intension. My vision was a bit blurry, my heart-rate greatly elevated, the very tip of my felt bowler lacerated, but I was otherwise fine.

Upon returning home, I presented the object to Holmes, along with a recount of my horrifying experience. He sat by our black fireplace, calmly smoking a cigarette as I related my story. To my great surprise, he, with its conclusion, indulged in a fit of wild laughter!

"I say, Watson, I must congratulate you upon coming so close to earning the dubious distinction of attaining the sixth tarot!"

The look of hurt and revulsion on my face stayed any further levity on the part of my companion.

"Oh, I am sorry, Watson, to make light of what must have been a terrifying incident. Truly I am. But, you see, you were never in any actual danger."

"I wasn't?" I asked in the manner of a confused child.

"Certainly not," my friend answered. "Had the verutum-wielding assailant meant to do you any harm he would surely have chosen a more practical means of execution than a replica of a pole weapon from the ancient world."

"I don't follow you, Holmes."

"Watson, my good fellow, I'm extremely fond of you, but you present a rather unworthy target for any serious assassin. You employ neither stealth nor vigilance. You hobble about in a mode of self-absorption and pensiveness, harmless as a meandering lamb. Were I intent upon removing Dr. John Watson from the scene, I would need nothing more than a sharp blade and a minor degree of isolation. Nor would I have assaulted you near the mouth of the alley, but, rather, would have let you trail further into it, and, once in its depths, would have dispatched you with little effort."

Had any other man given such a blood chilling hypothetical, I would have shuddered. However, being all too accustomed to the cold and calculating nature of Holmes' mind, I let the comment pass.

"But if there was no real intent to harm me, why stage such an incident?" I asked, eager to move the conversation along and not linger on such an unnerving subject.

At this query, my companions shrugged. "A futile attempt to unnerve me, I suppose. Do be more careful in the future, old man, but don't grey a hair on your head over your safety in this little adventure. Our present adversary is ruthless, but rational, and knows he stands nothing to gain by eliminating my chronicler. Believe me, my friend, if I thought for a moment your life was in any real danger, I'd decline any further aid from you and allow John Watson to return his attention wholly to the practice of his noble trade."

How crestfallen I became at this remark! I vaguely recollected how dull had been my life as a simple physician!

"Comes, Watson," said my friend, rising from his chair and casting his fag into the grate with gusto. "We shall yet turn the tables on this tarot dealer and avenge the injury done to your bowler! Let us off to the heart of London!"

***

Camden greeted us not one hour hence. We made our way down several narrow, crowded streets to the august office of Mr. Arwin Romanus, esquire. It was a glorious building of dark brick and wood, tall and erect as a sentinel standing at attention. We rang the knocker and were immediately admitted. A secretary, stern-faced as a stone bust of caesar and formal as an archbishop, graciously received us. After a short wait, a stiff, high-shouldered servant appeared and politely instructed us to follow him. He ushered us down a dark passage, through a blackened burgundy oaken door, and into an apartment almost intimidating by its very somberness. We were hastily announced, after which the door was tightly closed behind us. (One rather got the impression of being entombed!) The air was the scent of lavender and catmint.

Before us sat a large, ornate desk of dark mahogany, behind which was enthroned a person of such outward dignity and self-possession, that we could hardly forbear greeting him with the reverence reserved for men of high stature. The gentleman, impressively garbed in a dark grey suit of woolen serge and embroidered waistcoat, had the serious airs of a black-letter clergyman combined with a face that bespoke strong and shrewd faculties. He rose to receive us cordially, although, I feel compelled to note, he did so in the manner of a superior being just able to bear the intrusion of his lessers. I don't mind saying that I found the man intimidating.

"What can I do for you gentleman?" asked he, getting straight to business

"Thank you kindly for seeing us, Mr. Romanus. We're assisting the police in the investigation of the Richard Corkright murder and hoped we might take a little of your valuable time in order to collect some information."

"So I've been informed. Please do proceed," said he in measured tones.

"Firstly, what can you tell me about your dealings with Richard Corkright?"

"Corkright was a close personal friend. I knew him the whole of his life. We grew up together. I've been his solicitor for nigh two decades. We saw each other socially. We exchanged professionally courtesies. I witnessed for him and he for me. We referred clients to one another. That sort of thing. A genuine tragedy his premature loss is."

"You are to settle his estate next week?"

"The sad duty falls to me, yes, Monday next."

"Mr. Romanus, I am aware we are touching on a sensitive matter, but many lives have already been lost and more hang in the balance. What can you tell me of his will?"

"He filed a will with me not more than a year or so ago. I harped him about it for years. A man of his wealth, you know..."

"What caused him to relent after delaying so long?"

"Why, I'm not entirely sure, sir. It was not long after our mutual friend Renata Wakeham took ill. She's the widow of the late Paul Wakeham, friend to both Corkright and myself. Her declining health seemed to have made some impact on him."

"You three were close?"

"Oh, yes. Paul and myself were childhood chums, and made the acquaintance of Richard as college-age boys. We spent our salad days together."

"I'm curious: when is the last time the three of you were together?"

The honored gentleman took to polishing his spectacles as he threw his memory into action. "Let me think. I believe it would have been when Corkright and I visited Wakeham as he was convalescing from wounds received in the service."

"How did he come to be injured?"

"I believe he took a bullet during fighting in Baluchistan."

"Forgive my prying, but why was that the last time?"

"It was not long after this that Paul married. (Against the wishes of both families, I might add – the whole thing created quite a stir.) He had a wife to attend to and provide for, while Corkright and I remained bachelors. He became rather hard to keep up with after that."

"Why is that?"

"Well, you see, Mr. Holmes, my friend married somewhat above his station. Mrs. Wakeham, who was originally a Miss Bollinger, came from a wealthy family who own several large cotton plantations in Antigua and Barbuda. Paul wanted to keep her in the lifestyle to which she was accustomed. He turned to enterprise after enterprise trying to make his fortune, and was consequently always on the move."

"What line of work did he pursue?"

"He started, I believe, as an exporter in the swamps of Jahar, and later became a fabric dealer in Panay. After that little venture failed he moved to Spain –where was it? Oh, yes, in La Corinna, where he dealt in linens and other things. Finally, he ended up in the sugar industry in Laon, where he died, passing before the birth of his only child. Of a stroke, or so it appeared. So tragic."

"Did Richard Corkright maintain close ties to the Wakehams?"

"I believe he was a minor investor is some of Paul's ventures and visited them from time to time."

"And you say both families opposed the marriage?"

"Yes, but I never fully understood why. Paul was a fine man, and she a lovely woman. I do know that their families threatened to cut them off if they wed and made good their threat after they did."

"She must have made quite an impression on your friend."

"You mean to persuade him to leave the service, forsake his family and journey around world trying to build for her a fortune?"

"Exactly."

"It's true. He was, like myself and Corkright, a confirmed bachelor until he met her, the dark haired girl with a stately gait and a certain cock of her eyes. She was indeed a very charming young woman."

"Mr. Wakeham's buried in France?"

"Yes, so I am told. Never had the opportunity to go there and visit his grave."

"Had he any enemies in his business dealing?"

"Enemies, Mr. Holmes? What man doesn't have enemies? Rivals he had plenty, business competitors and the like. Certainly rivals for his fair bride while he courted her. Some stiff rivals, in fact. He was a person little understood and not always liked. But nothing could be said against his business integrity."

"And his personal integrity?"

"Nor that, so far as I am aware," answered our host, showing distain at the question.

"When did Wakeham die?"

"His son is fast twenty-seven, and he died before he was born."

"Do you recall the date?"

"I'm not entirely sure. It was nearly three decades ago. My recollection was it occurring in November. We were both lax Catholics, and I recall him jokingly mentioning the approach of the feast of St. Andrews in the last letter he sent me."

"His wife returned home immediately after his death?"

A servant entered the room with a tray of three tumblers of kirschwasser. Each of was presented with one.

"Renata returned shortly thereafter, somewhat discretely (his family nursing a grudge against her). She's got by on the Paul's meager pension and with help from friends. Forgive me, Mr. Holmes, but what has all this to do with the murder of Richard Corkright?"

"Possibly nothing in the world, Mr. Romanus, but I have found it useful in my line of work to gather information indiscriminately and parse later." Holmes paused to sip his drink. "You indicated that Corkright had been kind to Mrs. Wakeham. I take it, she never married again."

"No, never married again."

"Corkright never pursued her?"

The lawyer set his tumbler on the desk, a flash of indignation crossing his face.

"You fail to understand the situation, Mr. Holmes. Both Corkright and I hold the lady in the highest regard, as a friend. It was Corkright that paid for her to go to the continent after she took ill, and I who made the arrangements. At no small expense, we sent her to Kitzbuhel, to Davos, and finally over to Aix-les-Bains. We went to great pains to insure her total comfort. So you'll see why I find your question distasteful."

"Forgive me, Mr. Romanus, if I have given offense. I fully appreciate the esteemed devotion with which both you and Mr. Corkright befriended the lady. Have you found opportunities to be kind to her child?"

"Some. Corkright was a god-parent to the lad. He arranged for him to be trained as an architect."

I chimed in here. "It was he who did the remodeling of Mr. Corkright's office six months ago?"

"I believe that to be correct, Dr. Watson. The commission was given as a favor. Paul had little use for a remodeled office."

"So we have been lead to believe. What can you tell me of that young man?"

Our host paused.

"Mr. Holmes, I am a professional man and not in the habit of gossip or tale-bearing. But as you are here representing the police, I feel I must give a more honest account than I prefer. That young man, who lost his father before he was even born into this world, has known hardship. Paul Wakeham lost practically all of his savings in his ill-conceived business ventures and his wife and child were forced to get by on very little. With help from Corkright, the lad was apprenticed and entered the guild just this last year. But for his assistance, I'm not sure what would have become of that boy."

"Surely, Mrs. Wakeham's family was helpful to him?"

"Her family, as I understand it, has never recognized the child."

I was moved to comment. "Fatherless, unacknowledged, and nearly friendless! What a shame!"

"Aye, the lad suffered more than his fair share of hardship. But poor judgment only compounds misfortune. Even as he trained to be a professional man and raise his mother and himself out of poverty, he took to gambling. I happen to know that he came to owe a large sum. The account was settled some months ago with a second mortgage on his Sydenham home, but this, I fear, is only a short-term reprieve."

"Do you happen to know when the mortgage is due?"

"I'm not sure, but I believe it to be due soon."

"Has the young man no hope of repaying it?"

"None that I see, Mr. Holmes. Corkright and I discussed baling him out, but never came to a resolution. Now Richard's gone and I fear young Mr. Wakeham must learn a hard lesson. I'll help him how I can, but the home is likely lost."

"How very generous of you, Mr. Romanus, to concern yourself with the boy's welfare," said I.

"One does one best duty, Dr. Watson."

"The poor fellow seems all alone in the world. I wander who he turns to in his hour of mourning. Have the two of you spoken since Corkright's death?"

"No. He was not at the funeral. I'm told by a mutual acquaintance that he has become rather reclusive as of late."

"He lives alone?"

"As far as I know."

"Domestics?"

"Two, I believe. An old maid who helped raise the boy and her daughter. I must correct myself. I now recollect that the older lady passed away recently."

"She helped raise him? I would imagine he and the daughter are close."

"I'm sure I wouldn't know."

"Would you happen to know if the young man is in Corkright's will?"

"Richard talked of putting him in it, but feared the money would only bring the boy to greater ruin. I have not reviewed the will since it was filed, but to my recollection the beneficiaries are limited to three: Stewart Nuss, an enfeebled relation over in Blackwall, and Wakeham's secretary De Greek.

"De Greek?"

"Oh, yes. Corkright greatly valued the man's service, and made a modest provision for him. The better part of the estate, however, is to go to young Mr. Nuss - who, in my opinion, is the least deserving of the three, but I am only the servant in this matter."

Holmes rose from his chair. "And a fine servant I am sure. Dr. Watson and I thank you very much for your time."

Romanus nodded in gracious acknowledgment. He shook our hands. Then, after ringing for a servant to show us out, bid us a good day.

"Oh, just one final question, Mr. Romanus, if I may?"

The gentleman looked up from his desk.

"What would it take to delay the implementation of the will?"

The solicitor was a bit taken aback by the query. "To delay a will is most unusual, Mr. Holmes," he answered. "A court may order a delay in the event of any credible allegations of fraud or some other matter making the will moot, but I assure both you gentleman that all is in order with this will."

Holmes declared to our host his complete confidence in his assertion, and, once more bidding him a good afternoon, we followed the solicitor's servant to the door. Once outside, Holmes surprised me by rushing down the street. I struggled to keep pace with him

"Holmes, what is the matter?"

"Come along, Watson. I've fear I've made a terrible misjudgment. Not a moment to lose!"

"But what is the urgency?"

"Haste, Watson! Haste! We must make haste in our journey to Lewisham. Come along!"

I confess to being peeved. "Why such a blasted hurry after a three day delay? Surely the interview can wait a full hour?"

"I fear it cannot. And we're not to interview Phillip Wakeham. We're going to warn him!"

***

During the cab ride out to the south eastside of the city, my companion wore a visage of worry as I never saw before. It instilled in me a dreadful fear.

"I say, Holmes?"

"Yes, Watson? What is it?"

"What has happened to unnerve you so?"

My friend shook his head. "Oh, Watson, I fear I've committed a terrible mistake in delaying our visit to Phillip Wakeham. I put no stock in clairvoyance, but I have great faith in human intuition, which sometimes forms valid judgments only dimly understood by our intellects. Presently, mine foresees a menacing shadow falling over that vulnerable young man. If we find him alive and well I will count this a most profitable day."

Knowing no word of comfort that would be of any value to my rationalist companion, I held my peace for the remained of the journey. We arrived at Lewisham as the feverish day was now mostly spent and the atmosphere was slowly turning sweetly cool. Quickly paying our fare, we rushed to his threshold of the Wakeham residence.

The door we found to be locked. Rather frantically, we pounded on the door. Getting no response, we peeked through a window. An unnatural shadow within unnerved us sufficiently to emit gasp from us both. Having no recourse, we forced entry. Rushing inside, we made a horrible discovery: a body was hanging dead from a rope tied to a ceiling fixture. We knew it must be young Phillip Wakeham.

"Look here, Watson."

I looked to where Holmes gravely pointed. A folded paper sat on a nearby table. Holmes quickly read it, then offered it to me. I waved it away. Though I knew it to have a profound significance on our case, I presently had no deep interest in its contents. I sat down and allowed my racing heart to slow, my dizzy head to clear.

We had failed in our mission, and I was sick over it.

Chapter 7

A Visit from the Dead

The following morning I entered the dining room to find Holmes sitting at the table with a cup of coffee in hand, the very picture of gloom. He seemed to have aged a decade over night. An unattended plate of eggs and breakfast meat sat on the sideboard. It was a common practice of Mrs. Hudson to leave a dish there when Holmes refused a meal. Sweet Mrs. Hudson – the incurable optimist!

"Good morning, Holmes. Did you sleep?"

"Not a wink."

I shook my head. "Can't blame you. Death has snatched away a young man. A terrible loss!"

"A loss possibly preventable but for the folly of human arrogance."

"I hope you're not blaming yourself for another man's error in judgment."

"Watson, it was I who postponed an interview, against my better judgment and your better counsel. Wakeham was a babe navigating himself in precarious circumstances. Any word from me, kind or stern, might have tipped the scales upon which he weighed the ultimate question confronting mortals. And I must live with this knowledge for the rest of my days."

Such a sentiment flustered me greatly. "Nonsense, Holmes. Utter nonsense! The choices men make in life cannot be attributed to others anymore than their successes or failures credited to others. That young man showed a pattern of poor judgment."

Holmes showed no particular reaction to my argument.

"Do try to put it out of your mind. The case is over, you did your part. Best forget about it and move on to other matters. Find some more pleasant distraction, hem? The cricket season is newly underway and I for one look forward to some good matches."

My friend briefly rolled his eyes in my direction as I spoke, started to say something, but then, indulging in something like a sigh, returned to his vacant stare in no particular direction. What a distressing thing it was to see Sherlock Holmes despondent!

"Holmes, is there anything I can do for you? Perhaps a trip to the tobacconist?"

"Thank you, Watson. Maybe later."

"I know. I say, Holmes, would you like to hear my wretched attempt at poetry now?"

"By all means, Watson, if you like," said he, with little enthusiasm.

I took out my pad, cleared my throat. I indulged in a reconsideration, then held firm. "I call it 'Village in The

Coomb'. It's just a dabbling, you understand? Well. It begins:

Like ashes of mourning, purple twilight
Fell o'er hills scattered as black shards of steel
And valleys decked in winter flowers bright
As the darkening day reached its seal.

I looked at my friend for reaction. To my delight, some life came to his weary eyes. A smiled played on his lips.

"What a true friend you are, Watson!"

"Thank you kindly."

"To share such calamitous verse with me in my hour of need!"

"Calamitous!"

"Quite so, Watson."

"Come, Holmes..."

"I sincerely wish I could label it at least a mediocre feat, but it doesn't quite rise to that level."

My heart was sinking. "Well, what is wrong with it then?"

Now he was becoming animated again. "For one thing, there is the rhythm. Poetry is meant to flow, flow gracefully and naturally, pretty poetry like water over stones, haunting poetry like blood oozing from an opened vessel. Yours, old boy, is clunky, like chains scraping along an old stone floor. Secondly, the imagery lacks any real coherence. Poetic description should sweep over a vista, whereas your cranes the reader's neck from Heaven to Earth!"

"I 'm sure you've done better," said I bitterly, folding up my paper.

"Me? Nonsense. Unlike you, Watson, I haven't found the courage to make the attempt. Don't despair. The world has poets enough. The true dearth is for men of compassion and of decency. How fortunate it is to have men such as you!"

"Glad to be of service," I said, I'm sorry to say it was no without smoldering resentment.

"But tell me, Watson, truthfully: do you really suppose the case over?"

I started at the question.

"Good heavens, Holmes, I should say so! The young man confessed to the crime in his note before going to his final account. The documents, if not the money, are recovered. The police consider the matter closed. What sane man would not?"

"The police, I fear, approach the case with their usual careless alacrity. I, dear Watson, take a deeper scope of view. It is inconceivable to me that that troubled young man killed Richard Corkright. And there's still the matter of the tarot murders, which I am absolutely convinced are related. No, Watson, the game is not concluded until the queen is ensnared."

I sighed at this development. "Well, then. What theory have you to contradict all the evidence at hand?"

"I pride myself on being unhurried when it comes to forming theories, Watson. I prefer to take regular inventory of the case at hand and slowly piece the crime together."

"Then let us do so," I requested.

"To date, we have a wealthy man brutally strangled in his office, followed immediately by the introduction and a so-called Tarot killer, producer of five mutilated corpses. For motivated suspects we have a nit-wit of a dandy set to inherit a substantial fortune, a seemingly honorable and unimpeachable secretary and an enfeebled relative snugly residing in Tower Hamlets."

I listened carefully as I took my morning coffee. "Well, if you insist on a conspiracy, Holmes, I'd look closely at that young man in Bexley. Would you like some fresh coffee?"

"Perhaps," said he, not to the coffee but on the question of the nephew. "But I fear the true villain is a diabolical puppet master, one who I am sure this moment sits with a complacent smile upon his face, no doubt very happy with matters to date."

"And whom do you suspect that puppet master is, old friend?"

"I'm not entirely sure. We have a confluence of interests that meet at 14 McGeady Street in Merton."

"What do you plan to do?"

"Nor am I sure of that at present. I shall form a plan, one that must be flawless, and as no others lives are at immediate risk, I intend to take the proper time in its construction. I do say, Watson, may I now take you up on the earlier offer for a trip to the tobacconist's?"

And so I left on my errand, glad to see Holmes rather like his normal self, but a little fearful that his despair over the death of the young man may have impacted his sanity!

***

The next day, I returned to my hum-drum life and my hum-drum trade. I saw some patients and gave the best consultations a distracted mind could produce. The stifled suspense I suffered from, however, made me border on madness. My professional duties were done by late afternoon and I immediately headed home. The day's sun was high when I reached Baker Street. I made my way to the parlor, refreshed myself, had something to eat, and rested in my cozy walnut armchair. I drifted toward slumber when a knock at the door brought me out of my lofty thoughts and back into the world.

It was a telegram for Holmes. It read:

#1.Sydenham Apt. keys NOT accounted for.

#2.Side-door found locked but unlatched.

#3.August 22, 186-

McVay.

I tried to resume my nap, but unable, chose to read a book. Lost in its passages, I lost track of time. My reading was disturbed when I heard a visitor enter the room, and looked up to receive the greatest shock of my life! There, before me, stood Richard Corkright!

Now it was my own sanity I feared for!

"Greeting, Dr. Watson. God save you!" quoth he.

I almost fainted. The man grabbed me to steady me lest I fall out of my chair.

"Watson! Hold up, old boy, hold up! So sorry to have startled you."

I had never met Richard Corkright, but the voice was very familiar.

"Holmes! My goodness. What is the meaning of this?" This as I struggled to catch my breath and still my beating heart.

"This?" my friend laughed amusedly. "Surely, Watson, it has come to your attention that the final curtain on this dreary little drama of ours is about to rise and all the players must be in full effect!"

"Drama? Are you alright, Holmes?"

He laughed heartily. "Never felt better, Watson. Now, to alter our conversation slightly, would that happen to be for me?" He gestured to the paper on the table.

"What? Oh, yes, arrived for you a while ago."

"Just as I suspected." Said he upon reading it.

"You suspect the key was used to access that secret passage."

My friend made a reproachful noise. "Come, Watson, you're more clever than that. The key used to activate the secret passage is not to be confused with an ordinary house key. The absence of the key is perhaps innocent, as might be the other information, but, for the time, all three pieces fit into the puzzle as I have it set in my mind. I'd rather not elaborate at present."

"Anything I can do to help?"

"Not at the moment, no. I would, however, appreciate it if you could make yourself available Monday – for the whole day."

Chapter 8

A Diabolical Meeting

But our case would not wait until Monday! It intruded back into our life the very next day!

Friday it was. I took the day off from pursuing my vocation. It had been a busy and ghastly week and a premature conclusion to my workweek seemed in order. I was settled into the apartment, trying to occupying myself with menial tasks, when I heard a strange sound outside my door.

I arose from my chair and went over to the entrance. Mrs. Hudson appeared in the corridor. It seemed she had heard the disturbance as well. She gave a look of inquiry, but I held up a single digit to indicate that she should remain quiet for the moment. She covered her mouth with her hand in order to strictly obey my command. Our eyes rested upon the door. We both sensed someone lingering on the door step.

I quickly retrieved my revolver and, finding courage, threw open the door. To my relief, and I am sure to Mrs. Hudson's as well, the stoop was unoccupied. It was, however, not empty, for a small package sat upon the top step. I recovered it and shut the door.

"Everything alright, Dr. Watson," Mrs. Hudson asked in a feeble voice.

"What? Oh, of course, Mrs. Hudson. Likely a small remuneration from a patient of mine. No need for concern."

"Why the revolver, sir?" she asked.

"An over abundance of caution, I assure you. Please do return to whatever you were about."

She nodded, not entirely convinced but still relieved, and departed. I felt terrible lying to the old girl, but I would not have her worry if I could help it.

I sat down, and examined the object. It was a thick orange envelope. A portion was bumpy and I was sure a small roughly cylinder-like object was contained within. Curiosity yielding to my caution, I put it on the table and waited for Holmes to return home.

***

Holmes came through the door roughly two hours later. He immediately discerned the situation.

Without a word, he snatched up the package and opened it. He looked at me for a moment, then emptied the contents upon the bare table before us. It was a letter written in crude red letters and a small article wrapped in thick wax paper: a severed human finger! The *digitus minimus* to be exact. The tip was dipped in blood.

"Great Scot!" I declared, but Holmes silenced me with a motion.

"No need to startle Mrs. Hudson, Watson." And he read the note. Then he tossed it to me.

Its contents were:

Dear Mr. Holmes,

I am heartfully sorry for any inconvenience inflicted upon Dr. Watson. It was my hope to make a quick end for the honorable physician. My assassin has failed. This is his finger, the price he willingly paid for his error. Assure the good doctor that I regret to say that this is but a temporary reprieve. I warned you of my intention and hold firm to my threat.

You have but one hope of sparing your dear friend, and I am sure you will take it. Meet me at the old slaughterhouse outside Smithfield, out on old Entwhistle road. At the very stroke of midnight tonight. A coach shall arrive for you one hour hence. You refuse my hospitality at the risk of my displeasure – and wrath.

Sincerely,

The Tarot Master

"You're surely not going," I said.

"I surely am!"

"Holmes, you are mad!" I sputtered.

"Perhaps. But the stakes of declining are too high. The fiend, in order to save face, may feel obligated to make good on his threat. Besides, rejection will likely serve to delay the concluding of this matter. I know it is foolish. A lunatic is not to be trusted in any way. But, as I have already said, men of my profession are by nature gamblers."

"I am going," I said.

"No, you are not," he responded firmly. "I will not risk it. Besides, you would be in the way, old friend."

"Holmes," I responded, looking my friend in his eyes for emphasis. "I would do almost anything you requested. I think I have been faithful in all ways. But on this occasion I esteem my own judgment over yours. It is my intention to either go with you or see to it that you do not set foot outside the door!"

My companion smiled. "So be it, Watson."

**

We stood on the curb outside our apartment waiting for the hour to come. It did eventually and shortly after its arrival a cab appeared. It stopped before us. A rather older gentleman sat upon the seat, looking entirely ill at ease. He nodded and touched the brim of his hat, but said nothing.

"You are here to take me to Smithfield?' Holmes asked.

"Aye, sir," he responded in what I thought was a rather high tone. "A gentleman paid me to do so. A rather strange and stern gentleman. Would you mind climbing on board?"

We took our seats and shut our own door. But did not move.

"Begging your pardon, gentlemen, I was instructed only to bring one."

"You will take both of us, or neither," Holmes said flatly. The man made a gesture of silent distress, but held his peace. We were off.

"I say, driver," I called to him.

"Yes, sir?"

"Would you mind showing us your fingers?"

He held out on hand, then the other. All digits were accounted for.

"Thank you."

"A joke, sir?" he called to me.

"No. A precaution."

***

The shadows of deep night were all about when we turned onto old Entwhistle, a desolate, neglected country lane that struck me as likely tracing its origins back to the previous century (perhaps even its predecessor). The timing of our host in dispatching the cab was impeccable, for the cab pulled onto the ground of the abandoned slaughterhouse five 'til midnight.

We disembarked. As soon as we were clear of the coach, the driver made off at a mad dash. I yelled and started to make after it, but Holmes grabbed my shoulder.

"Watson, don't be a fool," he reprimanded. "You didn't expect the cabbie to wait for us, did you?"

"How are we to get home then?"

Holmes pulled his overcoat around him for warmth. "A ninety minute walk into town and a ride home in any carriage we can hire. How else? First matters first. Let us make our meeting – and survive it."

I clutched my revolver in my inside coat pocket. We made our way to the old structure. Passing through a dilapidated fence, a rectangular door greeted. With only a moment's hesitation, we made use of it.

"Careful, Watson," Holmes whispered in a voice so low I only barely made it out. "Our foe is at the height of desperation. The game is now under new rules."

A long, broad room opened before us soon. As we entered it, a voice rang out.

"Good of you to come, gentlemen!" said a loud, accented voice, from a direction not easily discerned.

"A pleasure to see you here, doctor. And yet I do not recall inviting you."

"I am here nevertheless," I answered.

"Come, Tarot Master," said Holmes firmly. "No more riddles. What is it that you want? Why have you summoned us to this dismal place at this dreary hour?"

The laugh was menacing and cold.

"Look upon the bench in the far corner!"

So we did, Holmes making the examination as I guarded his back.

"This is some find," noted Holmes.

I turned to see what it was he had uncovered. It was a small polished casket. He opened the lid. It was filled with a large quantity bank notes.

"What is this?" Holmes cried out.

"Your fee," replied the voice, still hidden. "A servant is worthy his wages, after all."

"What is I am being paid for exactly?" asked Holmes.

"Come, now, Mr. Holmes. No false modesty among friend! You have conducted yourself in exemplary manner. It would be a great disservice for there to be no compensation."

"In accepting it, I assume it is expected that my services end."

"Quite correct, Mr. Holmes. There are many other cases for the great investigator to pursue. And no small amount of indulgences to be purchases with your well-earned purse."

Holmes slammed the casket's lid shut, doing so with great emphasis. There was moment of heavy silence. Then a menacing laugh.

"I am very sorry you did that, Holmes. You are not as clever as I thought you. You surely know the price for refusing my kindness."

"It is not your kindness I refuse, but your cowardice. You offer me payment not out of respect but for fear that I am close to solving this case and ending your heinous criminal scheme Now, have we any other business to conduct here?"

Again, there was a laugh. Then another.

"No more business, gentlemen," he said, with a sense of feigned regret. "You are free to go. Good night!"

"Let us be off, Watson."

We made our way out by the way we had come. I looked in every direction for danger, my heart pounding. We made it to the door without incident.

"That was too easy, Holmes."

"It is not concluded yet, Watson. Come." We sought to exit the property. As we exited through the gate, there was a most unwelcome noise. Growling in the dark!

Discerning the noise to come from behind us, we immediately ran forward.

"This way, Watson!" he was directing me off the path and toward a line of trees to the right. I followed, but failed to understand his tactic. I should think it much wiser for us to continue down toward the country lane by which we had arrived.

As we came to the trees, which were widespread elms, figures, at least three, charged into view to our rear. Snarling canine forms closed in. I put forward my pistol.

"That will not due, Watson," said Holmes calmly. "Quickly now! You up this one, me up this."

And before I had even a chance for reply, he was climbing up one of the trees. I had nothing to do but climb up my own. To think a man over half a century crawling up a tree like a hair-cut-to-the-bone school boy!

We made it to the bough of our respective trees, when the dogs arrived, snapping and barking with all the bloodlust of a predator in the heat of the hunt. I have no doubt they would have rent us in piece could they reach us.

Safe we were, for the moment at least. But our situation was hardly resolved. I looked to my companion, but he was already working to improve our circumstances. He was climbing to the tree next to him by way of a long, high branch.

"Holmes, whatever are you doing?"

But he did not answer me. He continued over to the tree, then, plotting his course, he climbed to the tree next to him. Then I saw his objective. He was now in a tree adjacent to the fence surrounding the solitary building.

"Come, Watson," he called.

I made my way to the tree Holmes was in, though I was in no way able to replicate the deftness with which he had made the journey.

Dogs are not known for their sight. They searched the tree tops frantically for us, but seemed to be unclear of our exact location.

"Now what?" I asked, winded.

"Follow. And be as quick and quiet as possible!"

Holmes crawled out a branch hanging over the fence. He took firm hold of the branch and rolled over. He was suspended by his arms for a moment, then dropped to the ground, at least four meters below, landing with the grace of a cat. Then he ran in the opposite direction of the gate. I copied his actions, again in a slower and clumsier fashion than my friend.

The dogs, hungry for our blood, were confused at the situation. As we ran off to what I took for the backside of the slaughterhouse yard, they took a full minute, perhaps longer to figure out the need to pursue us through the fence gate. And we made full use of that short duration of time afforded us.

Holmes and I, running as quickly as our legs could bear us, were halted when we came upon a most unwelcome obstacle, another section of fence. This was in better shape than the section on the gate side. In pure desperation, we ran along the length of it, coming at last to a small gap. We forced our way through it. I went to run, but found Holmes was not beside me. He, brave soul that he was, had stayed to block the breach with a loose board laying on ground.

The dogs were again upon our tracks! I prompted Holmes to conclude his work. He did so and again we took to our heels. We ran as long as we could until exhaustion compelled us to slow down. Soon we fell to a regular pace, panting like horses at the conclusion of a twelve furlong race. The dogs' enraged barking, a terrible den in the night, fell far behind us. It seems the determined creatures were unable to resume their pursuit. Never in my life have I been happier for an adversary's failure as that night!

"How much money was in that container?" I asked, breaking our long silence. I had just caught my breath.

Holmes shrugged and took his time answering.

"I'd say at least Five thousand pounds. Perhaps more."

I laughed. "Not nearly enough for the great Sherlock Holmes!"

My friend remained somber. "Quite the contrary. It was enough. Enough to prove to me that we stand at the threshold of resolving this mystery. The inducement was offered in desperation. The conclusion of the matter is surely at hand – and not a moment too soon."

He was feeling the hem of my jacket, which, I just then noticed, had been torn, viciously rent by canine teeth. A reminder of the dangers of confronting the ruthless men that invariably align themselves against Sherlock Holmes.

Yes, I too was eager for the conclusion.

Chapter 9

A Trap Laid in the Devil's Tail

The two days until Monday seemed infinite, but the new week, though stubbornly slow in its advancement, eventually arrived. Refusing to elaborate, Holmes simply informed me we were to go to Camden. We departed about half past nine and arrived within the hour at the familiar office of Mr. Romanus. We shot past the confused doorman and burst into the solicitor's office. There were assembled Mr. Romanus, Stewart Nuss, kindly old Mr. De Greek, and an unfamiliar gentleman hunched over and huddled in layers of clothing (surely the sickly relative). All our suspects in one room! They all beheld Holmes and myself with looks of wonder and resentment. What could I do but doff my cap? Life with Sherlock Holmes is never dull!

"Good morning, gentleman. Please pardon this unavoidable intrusion," announced Holmes calmly.

"What is the meaning of this?" demanded Mr. Romanus in a startled tone.

"Terribly sorry to interrupt, Mr. Romanus, but this time I come before you as an agent of the court." And here he handed the lawyer a document which I had no knowledge of.

The solicitor took it and read it. "A writ of injunction? Who granted this?"

"It is, I believe, all there before you, Mr. Romanus."

He resumed reading it. "The testimony of Mr. Jack Hawks? Who the devil is Jack Hawks?"

"A gentleman who resides in Southwark near the Thames. It is a place, I am sure, Mr. Romanus, with which a gentleman of your lofty position has no familiarity."

Again, Romanus took to perusing the document. "A revised will?"

"So runs Mr. Hawks testimony."

Romanus set down the document. "I've never heard of such a thing. Not in all my years at the bar. This is preposterous."

Here young Mr. Nuss sounded off. "I'll say it is. You can't just write a bloomin' will in secret. You have to have witnesses and all that."

"Stewart, please," commanded Romanus.

"Quite correct, Mr. Nuss," said Holmes. "However, the court has made a decision that enforcement of Mr. Corkright's filed will shall be delayed until the police have made a good faith effort to locate the alleged revised will."

"How?"

"It is my understanding that they will search his home today and his office tomorrow."

Romanus' face was somewhat red by now. "This is absurd. I was the man's friend and his lawyer, If he had a modified will, he'd have told me and not any Mr. Hawks. And why did this – gentleman – take a week to come forward?"

"We can all be thankful he came forward at all, before any miscarriage of justice could take place."

"Mr. Holmes, the allegations here are slanderous. I take exception to them," commented Romanus, having yet again read further the document.

Nuss leapt up from his seat, the suspense it seemed too much for the young man. "What are you talking about, Romanus? What allegation?"

Roman impatiently gestured for Nuss to read for himself. He did so, pronouncing the text under his breath.

"Phillip Wakeham his son! Poppycock and rubbish. This is someone's idea of joke. I say you go on with the reading, Mr. Romanus."

Holmes shook his head. "Do so if you like, Mr. Romanus, but I'll have no choice but to report your defiance to the court post haste. You'll be made to answer for violating the injunction."

The man glared at Holmes. "Excuse my bluntness, Mr. Holmes, but how is any of this your business?"

"I do but act as a concerned citizen, Mr. Romanus. One who is interested, as I am sure you are, in seeing that this matter is conducted in a manner legal and just."

Young Mr. Nuss stamped his foot. "I tell you, Romanus, this here gentleman is up to some mischief or he's just plain mad. Go on with the reading!"

"Be Silent, Nuss!" rebuked the lawyer. "This gentleman is correct. We must all be servants of the law. The reading can wait a day until this matter is resolved."

"A sound decision, Mr. Romanus," commended Holmes, and doing so wished all a good day. And so we exited the way we had came.

***

That afternoon, Holmes having left on some secret errand, I had the unenviable task of keeping company with Inspector McVay. He arrived not long after Holmes left, showing the agitated disposition of a caged tiger. He smoked excessively, paced my rug relentlessly, all the while regularly consulting his Emery pocket watch. The good constable seemed incapable of letting his occupied mind be diverted for more than a moment or two at a time.

I have found the best way to dispel anxiety is to find pleasant business to occupy a restless mind. As luck would have it, there was that very afternoon a small fete on Kneller Street being held by the Chamerion Club. Their objective, as I recall, was to raise funds for assisting invalid children. I had had past dealings with them and possessed a standing invitation to all their affairs. I suggested to the inspector we make a brief appearance and he, with some friendly prodding, eventually agreed.

The good inspector and I arrived within the hour, somewhat disobeying convention as we arrived in the clothes we had been languishing in my apartment in. The event was open air and the weather accommodating. The company, mostly comprised of the extensive circle of the local MP, was well-intentioned but still of the mundane variety, the two adjectives equally applicable to the buffet provided. A predictable pompous event, bland to the utmost. It was, however, at least a change of scenery. The Inspector and I mostly kept our own company. His mood was little improved and I must confess that my manners were now also rather preemptory, as I was much preoccupied. We were mostly content to sip champagne by the black nightshade.

"So what news from the McVay house?" I asked randomly.

"My wife has finally compelled me to buy her a gas cooker," replied the Inspector.

"Has she?" I returned abstractly, my mind elsewhere. He likely would have received the same response had he informed me that his wife had compelled him to agree to move the entire family to one of the moons of Saturn.

"All the rage," he said. His finished his glass before responding. "My mother got along fine without one. And her mother before her. But modern women, I suppose, have elevated needs."

At that moment, something came to my recollection. "I hear there is a new blessing on its way."

"What's that? Oh, yes. I suppose I should have mentioned that before. Yes, it will be good to have a child about the place again. Anne and Peter are at school."

"How are they by the way?"

"Anne is a delight. Peter gets bad marks and is clumsy at every sport ever invented by man."

"Come Inspector," I laughed good-naturedly. "The lad comes from a fine lineage. He must excel at something!"

"Indeed! Goading his indulgent mother and his aunts into getting anything he desires. It is hardly the outlines of a promising career. And he has several times nearly gotten the same treatment from me. How he carries on when he doesn't get his way! I tell you, in my day boys knew nothing of such histrionics and self pity."

"Nor in mine."

The conversation went silent again until I asked him about the condition of his wife's father, whom I knew and held in high esteem.

"Still teaching at Fourah Bay," the Inspector answered, taking a moment to nod at an acquaintance who had that moment passed by us. "Plans on retiring in a year or two. I can't imagine what he will do with all that time on his hands."

"I shouldn't mind visiting him Freetown one day."

My companion made a derisive sound. "Harbor cities in the uncivilized world are to be strictly avoided, Dr. Watson, if one values ones health in even the smallest degree. Crime and disease. Corruption and heathen lawlessness. My father-in-law is a good man, and values his duties as a servant of God and Queen more than most. But he is also very much an intolerable idealist."

Then we fell into silence again for some time.

Finally the inspector spoke. "So, what exactly does the old dog have in mind for us tonight?"

I shrugged. "I have received little more instruction than you, Inspector. We are to receive final direction this evening after dinner by way of telegram."

"I do not care for these methods of Mr. Holmes," lamented the honorable constable.

"Nor I," I responded sympathetically. "But how can one argue with success?"

"How indeed."

We mingled a bit. Then, making our modest pledges and bidding farewell to our host, headed back to Baker Street.

***

That night, Inspector Padraic McVay of the Yard and Dr. John Watson of Baker Street, obeying the summons of the Great Detective, found themselves shivering in the cold night air behind a stack of mildew-encrusted crates in the now famous alley. Two uniformed members of the police stood nearby. The time was nearly midnight.

"I don't care for this, Dr. Watson," said the inspector, for the third or fourth time that night.

"It must be so, Inspector. Holmes has so decreed," was my response.

"In the first place, I doubt anyone will be foolish enough as to walk into such a flat-out and obvious trap as the one Holmes has devised. In the second, should anyone happen to show, Mr. Holmes is all alone and practically defenseless!"

"He is to be trusted implicitly in these matters," replied I. "Desperation sometimes leads even the most brilliant of men to stumble into plain snares. And alone the old chuckaboo may be, Inspector, but Sherlock Holmes is never defenseless.. Now let us be patient – and quiet."

Our patience was not much further tested, for not long after this exchange movement was seen at the mouth of the alley. The enclosed space about us was dark as pitch, but the entrance to the alley was fairly well lighted by a broad sheet of illumination emanating from nearby gas lamps. There, three figures materialized, walking with both a degree of stealth and also with seeming confidence. Venturing to the approximate spot where I knew the secret entrance to be, they replicated all the measures Holmes and I had but a week before, one of the men shouting out instructions and the others obeying. They soon produced the same hidden entrance we had. One shadow, the one clearly in charge of the party, entered, while the others waited outside.

The inspector and I were both tense as we watched, waiting for any sign of Holmes in distress. None, however, came. Within about seven or eight minutes of the episode's commencement (I could not see my watch, so I guess), the figure who had entered the dead lawyers office burst out. The inspector and I started to pursue the thief, but found such an effort quite unnecessary, as the dark-clad man ran, not away from us, but rather toward!

At close range, I recognized it to be none other than Stewart Nuss. His declaration to us was succinct.

"I wish to be taken into custody!"

"What!" boomed McVay, as he and I exchanged expressions of confusion.

"Please! I have a confession to make!" emphatically ejaculated the bewildered young man.

The young man was taken away (as were his two companions, surely hired hands ignorant of all relevant facts of the case). I, for my part, was consumed with questions, and yet was destined to go to bed without a single one of them being answered.

Chapter 10

Wherein Two Cases Are Fully Resolved At Once

Next morning Holmes, having just cause, broke his fast at the most appropriate meal, instilling in Mrs. Hudson a state of exceeding joyousness beyond description. I left my food untouched. My mind was far too unsettled for sustenance.

"Oh, Mr. Holmes! Anything else, sir?" said the delighted lady.

"That will do, Mrs. Hudson," said Holmes, wiping the corners of his mouth with his napkin. "Thank you kindly,"

With a reproachful look cast in my direction, the kind woman cleared the table and left us.

"I tell you, Watson, there is nothing quite like a substantial breakfast, especially after nearly a week of sustaining oneself on coffee and tobacco. Watson, my friend, you don't look quite yourself this fine March morning. What troubles you?"

"It was a difficult night, Holmes," I answered. "A long, difficult night. I am not sure I even slept. Night slowly blended into day. This case of ours – these two-cases-in-one - occupied my restless mind, and I have eagerly anticipated discussing it with you since we bid one another a hasty 'goodnight' last night – which, I must point out, was actually early this morning. When one dreads the morn, the minutes race toward it, but when one is eager for it how they tarry!"

My friend laughed sympathetically. "All will be made clear, Watson, just as I promised. All questions will be answered in due order. I, however, am convinced that you could put it all together yourself. It would be a good mental exercise." He sipped his coffee.

"I could try. But, first, please do clear up the matter of what took place in Corkright's office last night? What possessed that young rascal to charge outside in such terror and run straight into the arms of Inspector McVay? I shall never forget that pale, ghastly expression upon his face."

"You know the old saw, Watson. Naturally, the frightened young man saw a ghost! And no random apparition, but the spirit of his deceased uncle!"

"Holmes! You put on the make-up again!"

"Quite, Watson. Nor was it a profitless venture, for it compelled the young fellow to atone for his misdeeds."

"By which I assume you mean the murder of his uncle?"

"Do I? Shall we make a game of it, Watson? What do you suppose Mr. Nuss' confession to be? I shall listen in awe, like the disciple at the foot of the master."

"Well, I expect he confessed to being the mastermind of a conspiracy involving followers of those hideous Shrike brothers."

"Excellent, Watson. You did not overlook them!"

"That he, Stewart Nuss, devised a plan to rob his uncle, after whom he bore a petty grudge. He and the members of the disbanded Shrike gang, through wicked manipulation, compelled Phillip Wakeham to install the secret door during his renovation of Corkright's Merton office."

"Good, old fellow, so good! Keep going."

"Corkright was made to open the safe, but as the thieves sought to flee, he, desperate to protect the items entrusted to him, attacked one of them, provoking the intruder to slay him in the most quiet manner possible. The members of the Shrike gang were given their share of the loot, after which they fled the country. Nuss, meanwhile, stood to inherit a tidy sum, a portion of which I assume to have been given to Wakeham, as a warrant of silence."

"Magnificent, Watson! What happened next?"

"Philip Wakeham came to suffer from terrible remorse for his indirect participation in murder and opted for what he saw as the only noble recourse. In order to reclaim the laurel of honor, he took full responsibility for the crime, hiding his conspirators from the scope of the law."

"I'm all a-tingle, Watson! And what of that great meddler, Sherlock Holmes? I do hope his participation in the affair will be properly noted."

"It surely shall not! He, you, concocted fabricated testimony which delayed the reading of Richard Corkright's will which made Stewart Nuss fearfully contemplate the possibility of another will. With a quarter million pounds in the balance, he felt compelled to make one final usage of the secret alley entrance in an attempt to precede the police in its discovery."

"Your deductions astound me, sir! Your case is highly plausible, well reasoned and well articulated – and hopelessly wrong!"

"Wrong, did you say, Holmes?"

"Almost entirely, my good man."

I was simply dejected. "Then do tell me the truth of this miserable episode."

"Are you sure you want me to? I wouldn't want to spoil the fabulous account you'll no doubt read in this afternoon's paper."

"Curse you, Holmes! I won't be made to wait!"

Holmes laughed. "Fine, poor, fellow. I won't prolong your agony. Just wait for me to light my pipe. Ah, there. Now, where shall we begin?"

"With the confession of Stewart Nuss, of course."

"That? He confessed to being in league with a power more diabolical than any devotees of the Shrike brothers. The true architect of this devilish scheme was none other than Arwin Romanus!"

"My dear Holmes!"

"It was indeed he. It was during our delightful visit to his office that the true nature and scope of this affair became clear to me, for I found him to be, under all that charming and imposing refinement, a man dangerous and calculating. In his arrogance, he spoke rather freely with us, and by the conclusion of our interview I had what those who indulge in vernacular speech would assess a "gut feeling" that it was the Camden lawyer who stood at the center of the dark scheme."

"I just can't believe a man of his position-"

"Believe it, Watson. Do not be deceived by appearances. Not all criminals go about with dirty rags on their back, grease on their hands, and sneers on their lips. There are among even the highest strata of dashingly dressed gentlemen a class of men possessing the supreme intellects and ruthless instincts suited for the relentless pursuit of wealth, power, and revenge."

"Do go on, Holmes," I prompted after he fell silent in reflection.

"Bearing some mysterious grudge against Richard Corkright (the lovely Mrs. Renata Wakeham, I suspect, being at the center of which), and coveting Corkright's wealth, Romanus drew up his scheme. He prompted his friend for years to make a will, and when he finally relented, old Romanus entered into a conspiracy with Nuss to arrange, not merely for the robbery of his kinsman, but for his cold-blooded murder."

"Entirely heinous!"

"No interruptions from the audience or the ushers will remove the troublemakers! To continue, the execution of the first phase of the plan was quite simple, though rather clever. Philip Wakeham, an otherwise noble young fellow in a tight spot, was brought into the fold through desperate circumstances and not coarse manipulation as you supposed. He constructed the secret entrance, with the false understanding that it was to be used to conduct a simple robbery against his godparent, with all proceeds to be split seven ways."

"Seven ways, you said?"

"Seven, Watson. In addition to young Mr. Nuss and young Mr. Wakeham, an assassin, two to aid in the opening and closing of the entrance, and two to stage a distraction in the front of the establishment to engage the secretary and anybody else who should happen to be in the office at the time when the secret door was being opened and restored for the killer to exit– which, as you pointed out, would have created a great quantity of noise."

"Nuss recruited accomplices from his dog-fighting circle?"

"Correct, Watson. And each was given a task consistent with his skills. To the two down-and-out actors, the Newquist brothers, was given the task of staging a distraction on Corkright's stoop. The task of assassination was given to a freakish strong man, James Purvey, and the task of aiding him in entering and leaving the room given to his two cousins, the brothers Dornbeck.

"Let me try to get the whole thing straight in my mind, Holmes. The murder of Richard Corkright was intentional?"

"Quite. The robbery was a decoy, albeit, a rather lucrative one. The estate was the prize sought after. Thus, Corkright was quickly and quietly dispatched after opening his safe."

"But Mr. De Greek said that the place was disordered when he entered the room that day. If Corkright was killed in cold blood as you say, why was the room found to be in such a state of disarray?"

"I suspect the condition of the room had little if anything to do with the intruder. Ole Corkright likely upset his desk immediately upon entering his office that morning. (Remember, he was quite upset at the letter he had received.) The killer no doubt emerged from the corner during Corkright's tantrum and surprised him."

"I assumed that was the result of the struggle between Corkright and his murderer."

"What struggle would that be, Watson? You beheld Purvey with your own eyes down by the Lower Havering pond. Do you think it was any feat for a young man of his stature and strength to quickly and quietly dispatch a man substantially older and smaller than himself?"

"But tell me, Holmes, why would Philip Wakeham take responsibility for the affair?"

"That threw me off as well. But you see the confession we found on Philip Wakeham's parlor table was not his. A visitor arrived after the dark deed was completed and left a forgery."

"Who?"

"Our Mr. Nuss, of course."

"Stewart Nuss?"

"Be patient, Watson, and I will explain. The police, it will not surprise you to hear, were monitoring Mr. Wakeham in the days following Corkright's murder. According to the watchman assigned this task, a man meeting the description of Nuss visited Wakeham's residence several times. His last visit was on that dark Wednesday last week; he arrived around 11 am and left roughly half an hour later. Now, the household maid maintains that Wakeham was alive when she left the premises early afternoon, around one. The police agent, diligently maintaining his post in the shadows of the street, claims that Wakeham, to his knowledge, had no other visitors that day until our arrival later that afternoon."

"How did Nuss get in a second time without being spotted?"

"Well, what if I were to tell you that the police investigation of the deceased's dwelling found a home completely secured with the exceptions of the door we broke in our futile attempt to save the young man and an unlatched side-door. That is, it was locked but not latched, Watson. You gather the import of this detail?"

I sighed hopelessly. "Not until you properly explain it to me, Holmes."

"You see, Watson, Nuss, through frequent visits to the home, became familiar with the layout of the home. During his morning visit to the house, he managed to unlatch and unlock the side-door on the western side of the property. After the maid left, he made a second visit to the household on that day, this one considerably more discrete than the first, creeping into the house through the side-door, in some manner evading the notice of the police watchman on the street. I'm not certain what method he planned to use to forever silence his quarry, but it matters little. (Knowing the limitations of the young man, it was probably nothing more complicated that crushing his victim's skull with a heavy pipe or blowing out his brains with a pistol.)

In any event, when Stewart Nuss discovered, to his pleasant surprise we may be sure, that Philip Wakeham had spared him the trouble of removing him, he was left only with the task of producing a fabricated note, perhaps replacing an original. He then lighted upon the keys of the Departed and exited through the same side-door he came in by, leaving the house, with the exception of the single unfastened latch, completely secure and without any signs of intrusion. He assumed the police would not trouble themselves about a dead man's missing set of keys - and he was proven right!"

"And so now I understand the murderer's plan. But, come, Holmes, how do you know it was Nuss who crept into the home of Philip Wakeham, and not some other agent of wicked old Romanus?"

"Doesn't it stand to reason, Watson? Romanus wanted as few conspirators as possible in this enterprise. He intended to eliminate everyone of them and sought to minimize his task."

"My dear Holmes!"

"Watson, if you want to understand the criminal mind, you must forsake all sentimentality. There is seldom any honor among thieves. Romanus coveted the whole fortune and accordingly set into motion a plan to account for all who stood in his way."

I snapped my fingers. "Thus, the tarot murders."

"Exactly. They served as both a tidy distraction for the police as well as a convenient means of blotting out all accomplices. Portraying them as the work of some foreign agent was a nice touch."

"Were all the murders committed by Nuss?"

"You forget, Watson, Romanus already had a murderer in his employ in the person of Mr. Purvey. We can credit him with most of the slayings. Emboldened no doubt by the promises of Romanus, he murdered the Newquist brothers, and then, I am sure for the sake of extra consideration, was persuaded to shed the blood of his own kin, the Dornbeck brothers."

"Incredible, Holmes. And so hard to fathom. How could a man be compelled to such wickedness?"

"How, Watson? By the same greed that manifests itself in a thousand different heinous crimes every day in this sinful world of ours."

"Purvey, I take it, was done in by Nuss?"

"Good, Watson, now you're thinking like a reasonable criminal! Yes, Nuss arranged a meeting with the overly trusting executioner down by the Lower Havering pond, where he toasted him with a corrupted vessel."

"And why was Nuss spared?"

"Nuss had to be sparred, of course, until the will was read. The bulk of the fortune was to go to him. Had anything happened to him before the consummation of Richard Corkright's will, his share would have been forfeited to the other heirs. We may rest assured he had plans for our Nuss."

"Holmes! The carnival company!"

"Excellent, Watson! The perfect scam to take advantage of a greedy and not overly intelligent young men. I have a strong premonition that within a very short time of staking his investment and becoming the Vice President of the continental carnival company our lad would have met with some misfortune or another. Instead, we can take comfort in knowing him to be presently in a warm, safe cell, although a rope I'm sure will soon enough unsettle his neck."

"I can't help but think how things might have been different if only young Philip Wakeham had gone straight to the police after the murder was reported in the paper!"

"Or if only I, for that matter, had followed your excellent advice and not forestalled our visitation to Wakeham. Men's fates, however, are settled upon definitive actions (as well as inactions) and not the speculations of hindsight."

"Too true, Holmes. But I'm not sure I understand why Nuss took the better part of a week to eliminate Wakeham. I'd have thought it would be an immediate priority."

"Oh, it was, Watson. It was. There was, however a complication: her name was Marian MacBrain, Phillip Wakeham's maid. She was very loyal to her young master and refused to leave his side. It would appear that young Mr. Nuss deferred in giving younger Mr. Wakeham his share of the robbery money. With it, he might have saved his home from default, or, more prudently, perhaps even left the country in order to evade the police, whom he feared might tie him to the murder of his uncle. Without sufficient resources, however, he was mired in his present circumstances. Food and supplies were delivered to the home, and its inmates got by. Thus, Nuss had his prey trapped, but he was continually frustrated in his attempts to be alone with his intended victim for any significant length of time.

"He tried, through his numerous visits to the household, to lure Wakeham out of the home, no doubt using money as bait, but Wakeham wisely refused. Nuss was fully committed to Wakeham's demise, and the young lad was, to invoke the common phrase, living on borrowed time. Not quite being up to the task of a double homicide, Nuss had to invent a scheme to remove Miss MacBrain from the house. The young man no doubt strained his limited intellect and eventually came up with a scheme. Marian tells the police that Nuss (whom she knew by the alias of Charles Lovelace, but this is neither here nor there) had, during his Wednesday morning visit to the household, made her aware of a rather lucrative position currently open at the home of a friend in a country village on London's northern outskirts whose name is irrelevant. As a personal favor toward the lady, he claimed to have arranged an interview for her later that afternoon. He even went so far as to loan the cash strapped young woman money for the fare. She, however, arrived at the address to find that while there had recently been an open position, it had long since been filled."

"Strange that she fell for such a ploy."

"Do not be too harsh to the young lady. She knew her current situation would be coming to an end with the imminent foreclosing of Wakeham's home. It was an opportunity she could hardly afford to let slip by. Sadly, her departure likely convinced Wakeham that, having lost his last friend in the world, his situation was truly hopeless. Thus he ended his life shortly after she left."

"To address another aspect of the case, tell me, Holmes, who Mr. Jackie Hawks is and how you compelled him to falsely testify about a revised will?"

"Put simply, he is a bystander whom I duped. I'm not overly proud of it, but it was for the cause of justice, Watson. I disguised myself as the Richard Corkright, and, after a lengthy search, found a – vagabond is such an unpleasant word - an individual sufficiently, shall we say, removed from conventional society to render him unaware of recent events - or even, for that matter, the current course of the calendar! 'Richard Corkright' made a confession to the simple but attentive man. By a happy coincidence, Sherlock Holmes not an hour later came upon the simple gentleman and took down his testimony which he in turn submitted to the court."

"Clever, Holmes," I said with a triumphal clap of my hands. "Though nothing more than I've come to expect."

"Thank you, old man."

"Just to wrap up some ends, may I make a few miscellaneous queries?"

"A few? Make all you like!"

"I take it was Nuss that greeted us at the slaughterhouse?"

"Naturally. And it was he who supplied the perilous canines for our amusement."

"And the finger that was mailed us last week?"

"That is not too hard to account for. What morgue is well guarded?"

"Well, as I said, well done, Holmes. I several times found the case too complex – not to mention dangerous – to ever be successfully navigated. But I must find some fault with you in one thing."

"Then by all means do so, Watson, if you absolutely must. What is it?"

"I do not care for the maligning the reputation of Mrs. Renata Wakeham with that fantastic tale about Philip being Richard Corkright's secret son. Even accounting for the interests of justice, it strikes me as immoral deception."

"Ah, but, Watson, who is to truly say what is fantastic and what is factual?"

"My dear Holmes!"

"Nothing new under the sun, Watson. Do not let propriety or idealism blind you. Mrs. Wakeham was flesh and blood and subject to all mortal weaknesses. Corkright, quite handsome in his young days, was a frequent visitor to the Wakehams. And Paul Wakeham was a man exhausted and much preoccupied with business. One can see how such a scenarios might play out. According to Mr. Romanus' recollection, Paul Wakeham died around St. Andrew's feast day, which falls in late November. Renata's child was born in latter summer, making Paul Wakeham's paternity, if not impossible, rather dubious. It is my supposition that it was she who penned the letter to Richard Corkright which bore a continental postmark which the charming Mr. De Greek told us of and which brought upon Corkright's head so much distress."

"Why exactly did the letter from Mrs. Wakeham upset Corkright so?"

"The woman I assume to be dying. Presumably, she wishes to expire in her homeland and not foreign soil. I suspect that she stated her intention to return to England as well as her insistence that her offspring be provided for – perhaps even publically acknowledged. Now, how much of this information Romaus was privy to, I am not at all certain. (Corkright's conduct in the matter may be the source of Romanus' grievance against him, but this is pure conjecture on my part). It is possibly a coincidence that he threw into motion his plan on the eve of Mrs. Wakeham's return. I am, however, always disinclined to lean on coincidence."

"Pity the letter wasn't recovered. It could have validated your theory. What do you think ever happened to it?"

"I know exactly what happened to it. The poisonous epistle found its way into De Greek's fireplace."

"He confessed to it?"

"He didn't have to, Watson. The character of men like Mr. De Greek is easy to fathom. What else was a noble servant to do? He understood the letter to contain sensitive material, material he could not allow to be made public. Under similar circumstances, would you or I not render the same service?"

"I suppose the old boy did what his conscience commanded of him. Well, I for one am thrilled the whole affair is over. I can return my focus to the cricket matches. Wait a moment! Holmes, you rascal!"

"What is it, my fine fellow?"

"It just dawned upon me! The names you used to test Molly Sounders!"

"Yes, yes?"

"They were the roster for the Campden Hill franchise."

"Naturally, Watson. I enjoy the cricket matches as much as any bloke. It is a most pleasant diversion. I hear the roster is quite good this year. Perhaps I'll make a small wager on them with the payment I am to imminently receive from the Friends of Richard Corkright committee – half of which, you may be assured, is to be reserved for you for your invaluable assistance in this matter."

"Very handsome of you, old boy. Oh, one final thing, Holmes, before closing the books on this episode. Mrs. Hudson says you sent a package out this morning to Inspector McVay. She said you indicated it had some relevance to the case. She is too polite to inquire its meaning. I am not!"

"That? Just a present I ask the dear Inspector to deliver to Romanus who sits this moment, by the helpful testimony of Nuss, in accommodations to which I am afraid he is very unaccustomed. Just a silly keepsake, really. The climax to the series. A formal conclusion to the charade of the Tarot Killer. Recall victims one and two died by knife wounds and were given cards from the suit of swords. Three and four expired from blunt beatings and were thus assigned from the suit of rods. Purvey fell to a poisoned tumbler and was awarded the fifth of cups. Bearing all this in mind, what do you suppose I sent our friend Romanus?"

I considered the matter before responding.

"Would it be The Six of Coins?"

The confirmation of my guess was instantaneous, coming in the form of a familiar sly smile appearing upon the face of my companion.

THE END

Also from MX Publishing

MX Publishing is the world's largest specialist Sherlock Holmes publisher, with over a hundred titles and fifty authors creating the latest in Sherlock Holmes fiction and non-fiction.

From traditional short stories and novels to travel guides and quiz books, MX Publishing cater for all Holmes fans.

The collection includes leading titles such as *Benedict Cumberbatch In Transition* and *The Norwood Author* which won the 2011 Howlett Award (Sherlock Holmes Book of the Year).

MX Publishing also has one of the largest communities of Holmes fans on Facebook with regular contributions from dozens of authors.

www.mxpublishing.com

Also from MX Publishing

The Missing Authors Series

Sherlock Holmes and The Adventure of The Grinning Cat
Sherlock Holmes and The Nautilus Adventure
Sherlock Holmes and The Round Table Adventure

"Joseph Svec, III is brilliant in entwining two endearing and enduring classics of literature, blending the factual with the fantastical; the playful with the pensive; and the mischievous with the mysterious. We shall, all of us young and old, benefit with a cup of tea, a tranquil afternoon, and a copy of Sherlock Holmes, The Adventure of the Grinning Cat."
Amador County Holmes Hounds Sherlockian Society

www.mxpublishing.com

Also from MX Publishing

The American Literati Series

 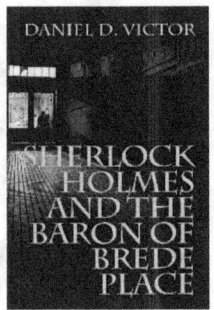 

The Final Page of Baker Street
The Baron of Brede Place
Seventeen Minutes To Baker Street

"The really amazing thing about this book is the author's ability to call up the 'essence' of both the Baker Street 'digs' of Holmes and Watson as well as that of the 'mean streets' of Marlowe's Los Angeles. Although none of the action takes place in either place, Holmes and Watson share a sense of camaraderie and self-confidence in facing threats and problems that also pervades many of the later tales in the Canon. Following their conversations and banter is a return to Edwardian England and its certainties and hope for the future. This is definitely the world before The Great War."
Philip K Jones

www.mxpublishing.com

Also from MX Publishing

The Detective and The Woman Series

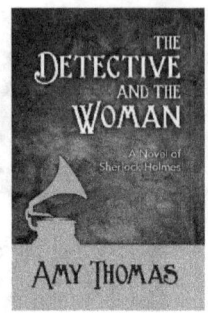  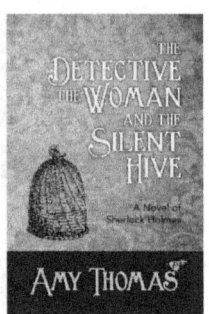

The Detective and The Woman
The Detective, The Woman and The Winking Tree
The Detective, The Woman and The Silent Hive

"The book is entertaining, puzzling and a lot of fun. I believe the author has hit on the only type of long-term relationship possible for Sherlock Holmes and Irene Adler. The details of the narrative only add force to the romantic defects we expect in both of them and their growth and development are truly marvelous to watch. This is not a love story. Instead, it is a coming-of-age tale starring two of our favorite characters."
Philip K Jones

www.mxpublishing.com

Also from MX Publishing

The Sherlock Holmes and Enoch Hale Series

The Amateur Executioner
The Poisoned Penman
The Egyptian Curse

"The Amateur Executioner: Enoch Hale Meets Sherlock Holmes", the first collaboration between Dan Andriacco and Kieran McMullen, concerns the possibility of a Fenian attack in London. Hale, a native Bostonian, is a reporter for London's Central News Syndicate - where, in 1920, Horace Harker is still a familiar figure, though far from revered. "The Amateur Executioner" takes us into an ambiguous and murky world where right and wrong aren't always distinguishable. I look forward to reading more about Enoch Hale."
Sherlock Holmes Society of London